MISTY'S TWILIGHT

OTHER BOOKS BY MARGUERITE HENRY

Justin Morgan Had a Horse
Misty of Chincoteague
King of the Wind
Sea Star: Orphan of Chincoteague
Born to Trot
Album of Horses
Brighty of the Grand Canyon
Black Gold
Five O'Clock Charlie
Stormy, Misty's Foal
White Stallion of Lipizza
Mustang: Wild Spirit of the West
San Domingo: The Medicine Hat Stallion

Misty's Twilight

by **Marguerite Henry**
illustrated by **Karen Haus Grandpré**

SCHOLASTIC INC.
New York Toronto London Auckland Sydney
Mexico City New Delhi Hong Kong Buenos Aires

ISBN-13: 978-0-545-04099-0
ISBN-10: 0-545-04099-X

Text copyright © 1992 by Marguerite Henry. Illustrations copyright © 1992 by Karen Haus Grandpré. All rights reserved. Published by Scholastic Inc., 557 Broadway, New York, NY 10012, by arrangement with Aladdin Paperbacks, Simon & Schuster Children's Publishing Division. SCHOLASTIC and associated logos are trademarks and/or registered trademarks of Scholastic Inc.

12 11 10 9 8 7 6 5 4 3 2   8 9 10 11 12/0

Printed in the U.S.A.   40

This edition first printing, September 2007

The text of this book was set in 12 pt. Baskerville.
The illustrations were done in pen and ink.

To Dr. Sandy Lynn Price
(owner of Misty's Twilight)
who warmed my heart by saying,
"Our book is like a dream
come full circle."

CONTENTS

This is the story of Twilight,

Misty of Chincoteague's

great-great grandfoal.

MISTY'S TWILIGHT

Chapter 1
THE DREAM

On an early Saturday in spring, when dreams explode into reality, Dr. Sandy Price tiptoed about her home on Stolen Hours Farm. She was gathering up research for the trip she'd planned ever since she was a ponytailed youngster in the sixth grade. That was the year she first read a book called *Misty of Chincoteague*, and the year one of her lifelong dreams had begun.

Sandy piled the breakfast nook table with a rainbow of color. The kitchen calendar topped the display, with a lively parade of ponies, wild and tame. Three glasses of freshly poured orange juice paled by comparison.

Thrilled with her production, Sandy stood back a

moment to admire it. She was interrupted by two sleepy-eyed children who came yawning into the room. Sandy announced the electrifying news: "All aboard for Chincoteague! What a glamorous way to spend your birthdays!" She picked up the calendar and with a dramatic flourish tore off April, May, and June and pointed to the last week in July. Chris and Pam stared.

Pam whispered, "Mom's flipped." But nothing could stop Sandy now. She circled the last week of July in red ink and called out:

"July 23 - Two birthdays and Departure Day, northward bound from Ocala, Florida, to Chincoteague, Virginia.

July 24 - Still heading north.

July 25 - Arrive Chincoteague Island.

July 26 - Scouting neighboring Assateague for wild ponies.

July 27 - The roundup and the swim across the channel.

July 28 - The auction."

Both children studied their mother as if she were a teacher dictating weeks of assignments. "Why, that's the middle of summer!" Chris said.

Sandy was deaf to the tone of his voice. She translated it as "That's so far away I can hardly wait."

"That's it," Pam said with a shrug of impatience. "It's done! July twenty-third—our birthday, Mom's D-Day."

The children shoved their chairs into place, gulped

their orange juice, ate their cereal in silence, and bolted out-of-doors.

All Pam could think of was the extra chores that would come with more horses. "Do I have to be a pony girl forever, weeding the racetrack and picking stones off it?" Pam wondered. Those were the chores she hated most.

Chris thought only of his snakes. "My boa constrictor is going to have babies in July. Maybe fifty! And Mom wants me to leave her behind for some dumb ponies?"

Inside, their mother remained at the table, lost in a happy daydream of wild ponies and crashing surf. In *Misty of Chincoteague* wise old Grandpa Beebe called one of the ponies "just a piece of wind and sky."

"Soon," Sandy promised herself, "some of those wild pieces of wind and sky will come to live right here on Stolen Hours Farm!"

Chapter 2
D-DAY

T hree months later, when D-Day finally arrived, the big thoroughbred trailer stood ready for loading. Sandy was up at sunrise directing operations.

"Pam, please bring in the empty water jugs and the pails. Chris! Can you lug a bale of hay and a bag of sawdust up the ramp?"

"'Course, but why?"

Pam explained, "Sawdust for footing, you dummy, and hay to feed the ponies."

Sandy laughed in gladness for the day. She felt an endless energy. She helped Chris pull the hay and sawdust up the ramp and against the trailer's wall.

"Now, who volunteers to clean two old and worn halters? They're hanging behind the door of the tack room; they'll be just the right size for two Chincoteague foals on their way to Stolen Hours Farm."

Each child pointed to the other.

"How about drawing straws?" Sandy suggested. "The short one wins the job." Ten minutes later Pam was standing on the bale of hay, hanging up the sweat-fragrant halters where they'd be ready at hand when they were needed.

Sandy nodded her approval. "Thank you, Pam. Now will you two run up to the house, grab your suitcases, and say good-bye to Judy. We're ready to hit the road."

While she waited for the children, Sandy climbed into the trailer. She pulled out a wisp of hay and began chewing on it, ruminating on how life shuffles us around. A child's world changes, she thought. Nothing stays the same . . . except maybe a dream.

Sandy had held on to her dream. The only other thing that had stayed the same in her life was her father's love. No, there were two things: Papa Ed's love, and his and her kinship with horses. From birth to old age, horses could be sad and glad, aching and frisky, jealous and angry—the whole gamut of ups and downs. Horses share so much with people, Sandy thought.

Her musings were cut off by the sounds of morning—the staccato hoofbeats of the yearling trainees, then the closer sounds of Chris and Pam grumbling.

"Who wants to go to a nerdy place with a nerdy name like Chicatig?" Unmistakably Chris.

Pam was agreeing. "And I was invited to a picnic with

Jan and Beth, and they were going to bake a birthday cake for me—all chocolate!"

"Big deal!" Chris scoffed. "What's an old birthday cake? My boa constrictor is going to have babies. She could have fifty, you know. What an awesome birthday present!" He paused. "Where the heck is Mom?"

Sandy sagged against the wall, scraping her cheek against the metal buckle of a halter. She barely felt the pain in the greater sting of disappointment. Her children didn't share her dream! They were going to Chincoteague out of duty! How could she have mistaken their real feelings?

Mechanically she straightened up, walked down the ramp, raised the gate, and shot the bolt into place. "Once we reach 'Chicatig,'" she said to herself, "the adventure will take over and they'll be fine." Then she quickly crossed her fingers, hoping she was right.

She climbed into the driver's seat and beeped the horn. Judy, the housekeeper, waved her apron and called, "Safe journey!" as the children stowed their baggage in the trailer.

Sandy circled the driveway and sang out in her strongest church voice the words to "Happy Birthday to You."

No response. No sound except the tires spitting crunchy gravel as they made the curve.

From the back seat Chris took off his cowboy hat and bopped it on Pam's head. His voice taunted:

"Happy birthday to you,
You live in a zoo
You look like a monkey
You smell like one, too!"

Pam turned around and made a face at Chris. "Thanks a bunch, baby brother. Hey, why are messing in the cooler?"

"Where's the cake?" Chris asked.

"Shh!" Pam scolded. "You don't eat birthday cake in a car!"

"What's the difference? You eat hamburgers and hot dogs in a car, don't you? Anyway, I'm hungry."

Sandy's face must have shown her stricken feelings, for Pam put her hand on her mother's arm. "Mom, don't feel sad. *I* don't need cake. Boys—they're always hungry."

Pam's words comforted Sandy. Her own excitement would not be stilled. It rose and fell with yo-yo resilience. She was on her way to collect her dream!

Chapter 3
MEMORIES RUN DEEP

Sandy skimmed through Georgia at top speed. She had taped a small map to the dashboard of the van showing the route from Ocala, Florida, through Georgia, and on up through the Carolinas to Virginia and the tiny offshore island of Chincoteague.

As the miles wore on, Pam and Chris began talking less about home and more about where and why they were going on this strange pilgrimage.

"How did the ponies really get to "'Chicatig'?" Chris asked.

"They were washed ashore from a wrecked Spanish galleon," Pam told him. "Don't you remember how, in the

11

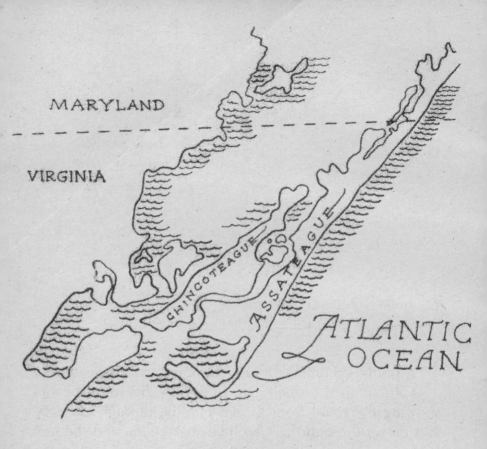

beginning of *Misty of Chincoteague*, they swam to a nearby island called Assateague? I don't remember what the name means. Mom, what does it mean?"

The question brought back a rush of memories to Sandy. All the scenes she recalled from the book made her eager to explain the purpose for this visit.

"Assateague is an Indian word for 'outrider.' It's a perfect name," she added, "because Assateague really does ride right outside Chincoteague Island, protecting it from the crashing winds and waves of the stormy Atlantic."

"Who protects 'Assatig'?" Chris interrupted.

"Assateague is a refuge of its own and a haven for wild ponies, white-tail deer, muskrats, migrating water birds, and the silver-gray Virginia squirrel, which is endangered," Sandy explained. "When we get to Chincoteague, maybe we'll even get to see some wild ponies thundering along Assateague's shoreline."

On the second day, as they were whisking through the Carolinas, the questions became even more lively.

"Mom, how did you hear about *Misty of Chincoteague* in the first place?" Pam asked.

Sandy smiled. How could she make the answer as exciting to her children as it had been to her? She slowed her pace a smidgen as she thought.

"I was just twelve," she began, "and there was a library close to school. Every Monday our class marched there, two by two, to take out an armful of books.

"Miss Paula Pepper was the librarian, and we kids liked her a lot. We had fun calling her Miss P.P. behind her back, but we didn't mean any harm by it. Well, one day Miss P.P. held out a well-worn book titled *Misty of Chincoteague*. She offered it to me with a kind of pride, then suddenly clutched it to her as if the pony on the

cover might run away. Then she said, 'Your impression might be that this a child's book because of the many illustrations, Sandy, but I want to tell you that people twelve years old and older check it out because it's adult in *concept.*'

"I liked the sound of that, and I liked the look of the little colt on the cover. Miss P.P. offered me the book a second time, and I took it eagerly. For the next week I lived with herds of wild ponies on a narrow barrier island called Assateague."

"And with the Beebes and Misty and her mother," Pam chimed in, excited. "What was Misty's mother's name, Mom? I forget."

"The Chincotoeaguers called her the Phantom," Sandy replied with a remembering smile, "because she was so elusive no one was sure she really existed. That is, until Paul Beebe caught her."

"That's right. I remember now!" cried Pam.

"I don't! Tell us again, Mom," Chris commanded.

So Sandy retold the story of *Misty of Chincoteague* to Pam and Chris: how the descendants of the ponies from the wrecked Spanish ship lived and flourished on Assateague Island; how two youngsters, Paul and Maureen Beebe, had fallen in love with the wild Phantom; how they determined to catch her and gentle her; and how they'd ended up with not just the Phantom but her tiny baby Misty as well. "You see, Misty was born only a short while before Pony Penning Day, and when the men came to round up the herd, she was so little and weak she couldn't keep up with the others. That's what slowed Phantom down, and that's how Paul caught her," Sandy explained.

"What's Pony Penning Day?" Chris broke in.

"Once a year, in July, the wild ponies are rounded up and driven into the channel at low tide; where they actually swim from Assateague Island to Chincoteague. Then the foals and yearlings are sold at auction."

In chorus, Pam and Chris asked, "You mean we're really going to buy some wild ponies?"

"That's the plan . . . if we're lucky. I've been putting

aside a nest egg for just this occasion. We'll bid on two foals, one for each of you.".

"Mom, how long have you been planning this?" Pam asked in astonishment.

Sandy smiled. "Ever since I first read the book."

From the backseat, Chris made a face at Pam in the mirror. "You know what?" he said. "Some moms never grow up!"

Pam nodded. For once they agreed.

Chapter 4

A LIVING LIKENESS

On the afternoon of the third day the big horse van was joined by a parade of traffic inching slowly over the causeway from mainland Virginia to the tiny island of Chincoteague.

Sandy clapped her hands on the steering wheel in amazement. "Look at the color!"

"Yeah, everywhere it's yellow-green," Chris said.

"Yes! Sea and sky to match the salt marsh grass."

From that moment of discovery—even before their wheels had touched the island itself—Chincoteague began working its magic.

Right away they checked in at Chef Jim Hanretta's

Channel Bass Inn, one of the finest little hostelries in Virginia.

"It's a good thing you folks have a reservation," the woman at the check-in desk told them. "We're full up with guests from all over the country. Why, there's a family here that's come all the way from Idaho, just to see Pony Penning Day!"

Sandy laughed. "I guess I'm not the only one who read *Misty of Chincoteague* and was inspired by it."

"No, ma'am," declared the check-in lady. "That little filly has a national fan club that just gets bigger every year."

Pam tugged at Sandy's arm with a worried frown. "Mom, what if there aren't enough wild ponies to go around?"

"I wouldn't worry about that," advised the check-in lady. "But please do be considerate of the wild things on Assateague. With so many people around, we have to be extra careful not to damage or disturb their refuge."

"That's right. That way we can be sure there'll be wild ponies on Assateague for many years to come," Sandy added.

Within the hour Sandy, Pam, and Chris had dumped their bags and were pony scouting on the sliver of land across the water called Assateague. It was just like the book had described it—wild beauty, pounding surf, turtles, and birds—except for the crowd of tourists straining to see ponies running wild and free. But there was not even a straggler in sight. Only some ospreys, snowy egrets, blue herons, snow geese—and the face of a red fox, plainly visible from a cleft in the dunes!

Travelers from far and near talked in small whispers, asking questions among themselves. "Do you s'pose," said Pam, "that the ponies are hiding in brush and bramble as if they know it's pony penning time and soon the firefighters'll be a-whoopin' and a-hollerin' and crackin' their whips to flush the foals out into the open?"

No one had the answer. Except Chris. As if he'd read the book of *Misty* just yesterday he said, "Old stallions probably remember other Pony Penning Days, so they drive the foals into hiding."

A man on horseback rode up to Sandy and looked directly at her. "Your boy," he said in a foghorn voice, "is dead right! Some stallions have seen a dozen or more roundups and know 'zackly what to expect." Slitting his eyes, he gazed over the eager crowd. "It'll be dark soon, folks," he called out. With a friendly wave he trotted his horse toward the short bridge to Chincoteague and was gone.

Impatiently Pam and Chris waded along the beach while the sun set, and a sickle of moon rose up out of the horizon, casting eerie shadows.

"Never mind," Sandy told them. "Action will come tomorrow. Let's head back."

They parked the trailer on Old Dominion Point, the little spit of land where Grandpa and Grandma Beebe and Paul and Maureen had lived. "This will be our vantage point tomorrow, where we can catch a glimpse of the ponies being rounded up and a close view of their swim across the channel to Chincoteague."

In spite of their eagerness for tomorrow they slept deeply in a big room at the Channel Bass Inn. When morning came, Pam and Chris felt the beginnings of excitement. They ate a Chincoteague breakfast of oyster fritters and golden squares of corn bread, and by seven o'clock they were slathered with sunscreen and ready to see the swim.

"You're way too early," said a redheaded native about Chris's age. "The ponies won't swim across till the tide ebbs bare." Then he grinned and added, "But you've got the best place to watch."

For once the reality was more exciting than the promise. The Chincoteaguers put on a Pony Penning Day that made their hairs quiver . . . a bunch of men who were fisherfolk yesterday turned cowboy today and staged the biggest Wild West Show in the East!

It was wild! It was mad! A hundred ponies were

driven into the sea by a handful of whooping, hollering, cap-waving men.

The water churned with ponies, and the air rang with the bugling of stallions calling their mares; mares neighing to their colts; and colts squealing in fright.

The swim across the narrow channel lasted only twelve minutes, but every minute seemed to take a lifetime. As soon as the ponies hit the water their white patches changed to spooky brown. They had all been sudsed and rinsed by the sea until their coats became one color—sleek and dark.

While the last swimmers were still scrabbling ashore, Pam and Chris ran alongside the pack as they were being driven down the main street of Chincoteague and into the pony penning grounds. By the time the ponies arrived, they were almost sun-dried; suddenly they were circus-colored pintos again!

But the loudspeaker was blasting the news for those who couldn't see. All the kids had to manage with only pinstripes of viewing between 80,000 human legs as close together as a picket fence. "Forty thousand visitors today!" a firefighter reported.

Chris and Pam were glad they were taller than most of the other kids. "It's a lucky thing we're ten and seven years tall," Pam said.

Slowly the roundup men and the parents watching

spread out to give more room for the kids to pin down their selections for tomorrow's auction.

"Mom! I've found three!" Pam was breathless with excitement. "How am I *ever* going to make up my mind?"

Sandy laughed. "It won't be easy. Even for me."

"Women!" Chris nearly choked on his gum. "Me? I'd just buy that little red colt, and we could get home in no time to see how my boa is doing."

Pam slithered in mockery.

Chris tried not to notice.

Pam said, "I want to do more than just look; I want to examine every single colt."

Sandy agreed. "And before we leave I intend to see every one of Misty's family."

"You said she was dead." This was Chris.

"She is! But not really. She lives on in her colts and grandcolts. Stormy, her third colt, is still very much alive."

"I heard that Misty is stuffed and mounted for everyone to see." This was Pam.

Chris looked scornful. "Who wants to see a stuffed horse with shiny eyes that can't even see?"

Sandy agreed with Chris. "Not I!" she said. "But I need to see her offspring. Perhaps there's one that's . . ."

"That's what?" came in chorus.

"*A living likeness.*"

Chapter 5
PONIES FOR SALE

At the carnival grounds on Chincoteague the pony pens swirled with action. In the big pen stallions were rounding up their mares, trying to keep them separated from other families; the mares were asking for trouble and trying to sneak away. A small pen held hungry foals, crying for their mothers and suckling any object within reach.

Pam was running between the pens, offering candy to the big ponies, who lipped them eagerly, in remembrance of other Pony Pennings when visitors had emptied their pockets of sweets. Pam giggled at the tickly feeling of pony lips on her hand. At the smaller pen, colts and fillies reached for the grasses offered, sniffed at them, then dropped them to earth untasted.

Chris kicked a fence post. "I want to go home," he said. "I hate this! If the firefighters own the ponies, why don't they feed 'em! How can they be so mean to hungry babies? *I* know what it means to be hungry."

Pam began crying louder than the foals.

"Pam! Chris!" Sandy's voice was firm. "Stop worrying! Don't you remember in the book when Paul and Maureen were upset by this very sight, they went to see the fire chief, and he said, 'Colts have got to grow up sometime. Their mothers can't tell a colt in so many words to go rustle his own living. They just kick him away, gentle-like at first. But sometimes they have to get a bit rough, especially when they'll be birthing a new foal in a few months.'"

Pam stopped crying. "I remember now," she said, "how the fire chief puffed up in pride at his parting words to Paul and Maureen. 'Separating the little ones from their mothers for only one night,' he said, 'why, that's the kindest way we know how to wean 'em.'"

A gathering of parents and kids were listening in. Chris and Pam reddened in embarrassment at the attention.

"Now," Sandy said, on a happy note, "let's take another

look at the babies to make sure of our choices at the auction tomorrow."

"I still want the little red one," Chris said. "Now we can go home and . . ."

"Just a minute, little brother. It's my birthday, too, you know. I've decided to get that little circus-lookin' filly. No, I guess I want the black-and-white one . . ."

"Women!" Chris sulked.

Sandy looked at her watch. "Heavens! It's two minutes to two. If we hurry," she said, "we can catch the first showing of the movie."

"What movie?"

"The movie *Misty*, of course."

All about them the fence rails suddenly emptied, and a surge of moms, dads, and children headed for *Roxy's*, where already a waiting line curved around the theater.

"It's just like Mann's Chinese Theater!" A youngster, wearing a T-shirt spelling Hollywood, California, pointed to a hoofprint in the cement. "Why, it's Misty's hoof," she squealed.

"Well, I'll be danged if 'tain't," a native Chincoteaguer exclaimed. He latched himself onto the little group, as friendly as a tour guide. "Y'see," he said, "I been working over on the main for twenty-odd years, but truth is, I'm a native-borned Chincoteaguer." A little audience began to gather in his spotlight. "Y'see a man could live here for nigh fifty year, but if he ain't borned on the island, he's allus a furriner. Come on into the theater. I'll show you what I mean."

What a relief getting away from the heat and mosquitoes and into the cushioned seats of the cool dark theater. The big screen opened with Paul Beebe running frantically to keep ahead of a stallion hot on his trail.

Their companion guffawed. "That's the fierce Pied Piper, leader of the wild herd!" he stage-whispered to the entire audience. "Piper's afeared Paul is trying to steal one of his mares."

The audience was running with Paul, screaming, "Run! Run! Run!" Hands were clapping with the organ music gaining power until suddenly Pied Piper was lost to view and Paul came tumbling down to safety.

The hour and a half flew. Everyone emerged from the theater, surprised to see the sun still shining.

Chris looked pleased. "Now we can go home."

"Not yet," Sandy chided. "We're off to the Chincoteague Pony Farm to see Misty's descendants."

The farm was on two-and-a-half acres of land on Maddox Boulevard, just minutes away from the theater. There were separate stalls for each of Misty's descendants. The family went from one to the other, listening to recordings:

"Meet Stormy, Misty's third foal, by Wings. She's still a lively one."

"Meet Cloudy; he's Misty's first grandson—out of Wisp O' Mist by Lightning."

What a contrast, these penned-up creatures, from the wild ponies of Assateague. Fame certainly had its price. A sadness came over Sandy that wouldn't be pushed away. She waited her turn to approach Paul Merritt, the owner. An idea was beginning to form in Sandy's mind of taking one of Misty's family home to set it free on Stolen Hours Farm. She took a deep breath and another. Then she braved herself to speak.

"Mr. Merritt!" she began, as if she'd rehearsed the whole idea. "Would you be willing to sell me that pinto filly—the one over yonder being groomed by a nice young man?"

"That 'nice young man' is my son, Greg," he said. "The filly's name is Sunshine. Come meet her and Greg. Sunshine loves to be currycombed."

There was no question about it. Sunshine was leaning against the brush as if she couldn't get enough of the warm, scratchy feeling. Her eyes took no notice of the milling tourists. She seemed to be living in another time and place.

"Is she thinking of Assateague and her wild friends?" Pam asked of Greg.

"That's probably the very case. She's homesick," Greg replied.

To Sandy's amazement she found herself quite out of breath. "Could my children and I . . . that is, could we buy Sunshine and take her home? We have plenty of room in our trailer," she added.

Mr. Merritt pursed his lips in thought and rolled his eyes heavenward. "At the auction tomorrow," he said, "you might better find yourselves a little wild one to take home. Besides, I have to mull this over. . . . You see, I got a lot of money invested in Sunshine. When Grandpa Beebe died, I took on all of Misty's family, fed 'em and gave 'em a nice place to stay. I'll mull a bit and give you your answer after the auction tomorrow.

"Meanwhile, how would you folks like to step into our little museum and see Misty, Sunshine's famous great-grandmother?"

"Does he mean the stuffed Misty?" whispered Pam.

"Yes, indeed," Mr. Merritt agreed with a note of pride.

Sandy apologized. "I'm sorry, but I just can't make myself see the stuffed Misty. In my mind she'll always be alive."

Chris grabbed Pam's hand and pulled her into the museum while Sandy took a step closer to Sunshine. "If tomorrow's answer is 'yes,'" she promised the mare, "you'll never know a bit or bridle and you'll run barefoot on our cool green pasture with a creek of fresh running water."

Sunshine was not even listening, and Mr. Merritt was lost in the maze of visitors.

Sandy gathered up her children. Stabs of hunger united them again, and they trooped into the Pony Pines Restaurant and ate a delicious supper of chicken potpie. The chef said, "Yer in luck, folks. Just three bowls left of Grandma Beebe's special recipe."

They ate in hungry silence, their minds reaching ahead for tomorrow's auction.

Chapter 6
THE "SOLD" TAG

The auctioneer was a burly man with a rollicking voice. He stood on a high platform like some benevolent creature smiling down upon his flock of eager children and not-so-eager adults.

A ramp led from the pony pen where the volunteer firefighters lifted one thrashing pony at a time and carried it up the ramp to the platform. As the auctioneer spoke softly and stroked the frightened foals, he seemed to hypnotize them into standing up straight on their spindly legs. Then he'd steady them and with a triumphant smile turn to his audience.

"What am I offered for this young'un with the remarkable

resemblance to Misty?" With his finger he traced the tiny map on the creature's withers, and to the howling delight of the audience, the little fellow turned to suckle the man's finger. The auctioneer didn't mind a whit. "This proves that the little feller has brains, spirit, and a sharp appetite."

The bids came fast.

"I'll give you fifty."

"Seventy-five."

"One hundred even."

A long pause. The offers grew in tens and twenties to reach $275, then stopped.

"*S-o-l-d*," the auctioneer cried as a ponytailed youngster exploded from the audience with her father in tow to meet her prize and tie on the "sold" tag.

As Chris whistled excitedly, his red pony, with legs kicking wildly, was carried to the auctioneer.

Everyone strained to hear the conversation between the auctioneer and Little Red, but they couldn't catch so much as a syllable. Again the charm worked. With scarcely any support from the firefighters, the little fellow wobbled to his feet.

"He's just a baby," the auctioneer pronounced, and made a pretense of looking at Red's teeth.

"Bid, Mom, bid!" Chris was poking Sandy.

People wanted to hear more from the auctioneer, but Chris, in the highest voice he could muster, called out, "My mom offers twenty-five dollars."

Sandy laughed and picked up her cue. "Make it fifty dollars," she called out.

The man behind her raised his hand. "Stud colts usually sell for less than fillies. I offer $150."

The bidding stopped abruptly at Sandy's offer of $200. Chris had won his colt.

The auctioneer spoke directly to Chris. "What a great sire he'll make!"

The crowd clapped and chanted, "We want a filly! We want a filly!" The bidding sharpened when Pam's Pie, a splashy black-and-white pinto, was pushed up the ramp on her own four legs. She made a pretty little jump onto the platform to everyone's delight. The bids came fast and finally stopped with Sandy's offer of $375.

Instead of considering their missions accomplished, though, Sandy was saying to herself, "Chris at seven, Pam at ten, and I, their mom at thirty-five and the biggest kid of all—am I to be left out? No indeed!"

During the bidding her heart had latched onto a little spitfire of a three-week-old foal . . . a miniature model of the fierce Pied Piper they'd seen chasing Paul Beebe in the movie. There was such a dear feistiness about him that it challenged Sandy. He'd be like a precious patient that called for all the skills at a doctor's command. But, at his tender age, would he be auctioned?

As the bidding opened, the fire chief appeared on the platform with the auctioneer and took joint command. The chief's voice boomed out. "This is an unprecedented occasion and calls for a debate: Should anyone be allowed to buy so young a colt as this little Pied Piper?"

Pam reached for Sandy's hand and squeezed it in sympathy.

"You are all horse lovers," the chief continued. "I value your opinion as to whether this little feller should be sold . . ."

"Gads!" The "borned-Chincoteaguer" from the day before jumped into the fray. "To my mind 'twould be kinder to send him back to Assateague to be with his mama."

There was a murmur of approval.

Next a very officious man faced the chief. "I've a string of young horses of my own, and I'm aware of how fragile they are. Stress can be a killer. This pony might not stand another swim across the channel."

"Is it possible?" Sandy's voice came clear. "Could we have the baby and his mother, too?"

The chief shook his head. "Sorry, but we can't let the mother go. She's needed as a brood mare."

A tall, sunburned man stood up to his full six feet four

inches. "I'm a veterinarian from over on the main." Everyone quieted to catch his words. "My concern is that the little fellow, if returned to Assateague, might be infected by flies and mosquitoes, which this year have reached epidemic proportions."

The auctioneer, who had remained quiet until then, addressed the fire chief. "Leonard," he said, using the chief's first name, "how about putting the situation to a vote?"

"Splendid!" the chief agreed. "Let's hear applause from those who want the little lady to take the baby under her wing."

There was a trickle of applause.

"Her children already have a Chincoteague pony apiece," the chief continued, "so the Pied Piper . . . why, he'll have a little herd of Chincoteaguers to make him feel at home."

"Yea!" the kids shouted.

"And my mom's a doctor," Chris added. "She'll take good care of him."

Nobody else bid.

And the little Pied Piper belonged to Doctor Sandy Price, who tried to say thank you, but the voters were clapping with such vigor they couldn't have heard her anyway. She gave a gift offering to the firefighters. Then, with "sold" tags tied securely about the necks of Chris's

Patches, Pam's Pie, and Mom's Pied Piper, they left to keep their appointment with Mr. Merritt at the Chincoteague Pony Farm.

Pam tugged at Sandy's sleeve. "Mom, do you *really* want another pony?"

Sandy gulped out her happiness. "Of course I do . . . Sunshine is almost three. She can act as Pied Piper's mother."

"But she wouldn't have any milk."

"I know. We can buy milk, but Sunshine can mother him with nuzzlings and lickings with her washcloth of a tongue."

They jostled through the friendly crowds going in and out of gift shops bearing copies of *Misty of Chincoteague*. There was a milling crowd, too, at the Chincoteague Pony Farm. But Mr. Merritt came right over, extending his hand. "I've been thinking about whether to let Sunshine go, and something tells me there might never be another family who would give her as good a home as you will."

Even the wildest dreams can come true after all.

The rest of the day called for a burst of activity— Sandy's family dashed up and down Main Street, getting health certificates, milk supplements, and extra buckets and shopping without luck for nursing bottles. They ended up with rubber gloves instead. That night they all took turns pricking tiny holes in the fingers of a whole box full of gloves, hoping that Pied Piper would suckle as happily as if he'd found his own mother.

It was almost midnight when they crawled into their beds, too tired to think about tomorrow's problems. The whisper of the wind and the lapping of the waves on the shore were all the lullaby they needed.

Chapter 7
FASTEN YOUR SEAT BELTS!

The loading scene early the next morning was something to behold. "Psst! They must be professional truckers," a passerby remarked about the trio. If the truth be known, it was the desperation to get little Piper home *alive* that fueled Chris's, Pam's, and Sandy's strength.

They stowed hay, grain, buckets, lead ropes, and duffel bags in the truck bed. Then, one at a time, each animal climbed in. The foals balked at the prospect of climbing the ramp and being swallowed up by the giant maw of a tunnel. Only Sunshine seemed fearless. Almost daintily she tiptoed aboard. Her whole attitude said, "Climbing into trailers is old stuff for me."

Pied Piper II came next. "He's so little," Sandy said. "Let's take him way up front in the airy storage compartment." The little guy followed meekly after Sunshine, but when he had to go past her into his own quarters he jammed on all four brakes.

With only a little puffing Sandy lifted him into place just as she'd seen the cowboy-firefighter move ponies at the auction.

"Mom!" gasped Pam. "How did you do that?"

"Love," she replied with a wink.

Chris's Patches had a mind of his own. He fought until both he and Chris were worn out. Finally Patches scrambled aboard with a snort that said, "Boy, you won this time, but just you wait, kid."

Chris sneered in superiority at Pam as she began fastening a lead rope to Pie. "She'll be a piece of cake," he said. "Fillies are always easier to handle."

Pam was taking no chances. "Come along, little dogie, come along . . ." she sang in her high soprano. Chris's prophecy came startlingly true, though. Pie was so impatient to join her Chincoteague family that she took her place in the trailer as if it had been marked in chalk with a *X.*

At last they were all packed in place: Sunshine on one side of the partition, Patches and Pam's Pie on the other, and little Piper already asleep in the front compartment. Sandy closed and bolted the gate.

"All aboard!" she cried. "Fasten your seat belts!"

They were finally on their way, singing "Home, Home on the Range."

Sandy sang her loudest, as if all her prayers and dreams from childhood had been answered. But it was like whistling in the dark. She was worried, fearfully worried, about little Piper. He was getting no nutrition

whatsoever. The night before, and that very morning, he had refused to siphon his milk from the rubber gloves. He had even rejected Sandy's fingers soaked in milk and all other acts of friendly persuasion.

"I should have known better!" Sandy said aloud. "A suckling baby should not be taken from its mother, no matter what the odds are."

"Yeah," Chris agreed. "If Grandpa Beebe was alive he'd have stamped his foot and said, 'I ain't a-going to let you do it.'" Pam looked at Sandy with tears spilling down her cheeks. "Mom," she sobbed, "should we take him back? What if he never eats?" But it was too late. The decision had been made.

At last, eight stops later, their temperamental Piper, ignoring the gloves as usual, plunged his whole head into the bucket of milk almost up to his eyes, and took three big guzzles. Then, with milk dripping from his whiskers, he blinked and looked up at his audience as if to say, "What's the fuss about? Don't you know this is the way it's done?"

Twenty hours later, with all occupants safe but exhausted, the van pulled up in front of the pasture at Stolen Hours Farm. Chris was first out, mumbling about his boa babies. Robert, the thoroughbreds' trainer, came running from the stable. He gave a yodel of welcome, then fell into silence as he opened the tailgate. His jaw hung wide for seconds, then he let out a steam-whistle bray. "Ye gods, Doc, was this a four-for-one special for the biggest spender?"

Pam answered for Sandy. "You know *Mom* . . . if one pony is good, let's take four."

Robert was still shaking his head as he lowered the gate.

Sandy said, "Please, Robert, will you get the little sorrel on the left? Then I'll back Sunshine out." Sunshine needed no help. She flew down the ramp and made a beeline for lush green grass—to sniff and taste and roll in its coolness.

Pam was already inside the trailer with her arms around Pie, talking to her and keeping her and Patches from following blindly after Sunshine.

"Pie, meet Robert," Pam said. "You better be nice to him. He's our boss man. Patches belongs to Chris."

Sandy went to her baby Pied Piper in his quarters up front. She expected to see him crumpled in a state of exhaustion. Instead he was up on his feet looking fresher than any of them.

Robert chuckled and quietly took over. "I've the makings of a hot bran mash for the big one," he said, "and plenty of milk supplement for the little one. The others can have the run of the pasture."

"Bless you, Robert," Sandy said, just as Chris came tearing around the corner of the house shouting his news.

"I've got a whole mess of baby boas! I counted at least forty five!"

"Hmmph . . . we've got *exactly* four ponies, lots bigger'n your yucky old worms," Pam said.

Chapter 8
SUNSHINE

The morning after their return from Chincoteague happened to be a Sunday. With four new Chincoteague ponies there'd be visitors aplenty, but Sandy's first task was to see how Piper and Sunshine had survived the night. As she approached their stall she softly called out their names. Her breath caught in her throat when Sunshine's beautiful head shot up over the half door.

Sandy peered inside and stifled a giggle. For the second time in their brief acquaintance Piper looked up with milk dribbling from his whiskers. He was alerted. His ears swiveled. Then he kicked his milk bucket out of the way and ran to Sunshine. Already they'd formed a loving bond!

Sandy let them out to pasture. Robert was standing at the gate to the big pasture with its gleaming pool. Piper and Sunshine entered as if to the manor born. The air went wild with whinnies and buglings of welcome. Piper pranced around the little herd, then stopped short. His nostrils flared to sift and sort a new smell. Suddenly he whirled and plunged into the pool, aiming for a huddle of ducks splashing on the other side.

Robert yanked off his boots and dashed to the rescue. He scooped Piper out of the water and plopped him in the grass. Piper was decidedly vexed. Plainer than any words he snorted, "You-you-don't you know I swam the Chincoteague Channel?"

Sandy rocked with laughter and explained pony penning to Robert. Finally he laughed, too, and they quieted to absorb the panorama before them. What spectacular splashes of color and action on the green!

Word of the Chincoteaguers spread fast. Clayton O'Quinn, one of their neighbors from Grosse Pointe Stud Farm, was the first to show up for a look-see at the new ponies. He was a very knowledgeable and respected horse breeder in the South. He made a quick assessment of the new arrivals and settled his interest on Sunshine.

"She's a fine-looking mare, Sandy," he declared. "A fine-looking mare indeed!"

· · ·

Days—then months—raced by, seasons blending together in a blur of constant activity. Sandy spent as much time with Sunshine, Piper, and the other ponies as she could, but her medical practice and the demands of running the thoroughbreds' training program kept her so busy! She often felt there simply weren't enough hours in the day.

Before she knew it, spring had rolled around once again. Springtime in Ocala was Sandy's favorite time of the year—the time when she saved alternate Sundays for visiting other horse farms to see the offspring of new stallions. Each new thoroughbred foal brings another chance for a great racehorse. Hope and anticipation run high as two-year-olds leave for the track. Gangling yearlings shed their winter coats and hint at the promise ahead. Stallions rear up snorting and bugling whenever a horse trainer pulls up in front of the stable.

One Sunday when it was Sandy's turn to go a-visiting, her last stop was Clayton O'Quinn's stud farm. It was a sultry day, warm even for Florida at that time of year, and a glass of iced tea laced with lemon had never tasted so delicious.

As they sat and sipped, O'Quinn startled Sandy by saying, "I'm interested in hearing Sunshine's story."

Her heart began to race. If someone of O'Quinn's stature appreciated their Chincoteague prize, he was entitled to the full story. Her answer tumbled out in a rush. It was probably long-winded and disjointed, but Clayton's reply was delivered with quiet slowness and intensity, as if it had been brewing for some time.

"What would you think of breeding Sunshine to one of my quarter horses or thoroughbred stallions?"

Her choice was instantaneous. "A thoroughbred, of course!" she said. "What a combination!"

As they walked up and down the rows in the stallion barn, Sandy was like a child in a candy store. She read the names: Heritage . . . Distinction . . . New Prospect . . . Big Bluffer. She studied the stallions. All were powerful. All had great conformation. Each could give his offspring speed and heart. What a dilemma!

She stopped longest in front of Big Bluffer's stall. "Why, he's the son of Bold Ruler," Sandy exclaimed. "Bold Ruler was a bright bay with a whisper of red. So his son, Big Bluffer, might intensify the color of Sunshine's colt."

O'Quinn interrupted. "If you can tolerate my boasting," he said, "Bluffer's *action* is far more exciting than his color. Even in play, his getaway is clean and fluid, as if he had to win every skirmish."

Suddenly Sandy bit her lips, thinking of the $10,000 stud fee.

Clayton laughed. "I know what you're thinking. This time, Sandy, your Sunshine will have a freebie with a pedigree."

The choice of Big Bluffer seemed to please Sunshine, too. They mated late in October. Three months later, a veterinarian examined her and solemnly made his pronouncement: "Sunshine is definitely in foal."

The early months of her pregnancy went by happily, but by the tenth month a nagging worry had crept into Sandy's heart. Sunshine's belly was enormous . . . and still growing! Had the big, brawny son of Bold Ruler been the wise choice of mate for their delicate girl?

Chapter 9
I'M A FILLY!

Stolen Hours Farm was a strange mixture of creatures. The thoroughbreds were the solid, pay-the-bills residents. On the other side of the fence were the frisky, frolicking wild ones—the Chincoteague ponies, like bright jewels on green velvet. Each group contributed to the beauty of the other.

One autumn morning at five, Sandy's bedside phone played a duet with her alarm clock. Andrew, the farm manager, sounded distressed. "I'm sorry to bother you so early," he said, "but I can't go with you to the Keeneland auction this year. Too much going on here . . . we have more buyers coming in from out of state."

"I understand, Andrew. Any special requests?"

"Yes! We need at least three yearlings. We could actually use three or four. Have a good trip, Doc. You're the one with the sure eye; you won't need me."

The September Yearling Sales at Keeneland, Kentucky, were an exciting assignment for Sandy. She had no hesitation about leaving home because the children were in school, and Judy was there after school. As for Sunshine, she was contented and not due to foal until October.

The moment she landed and joined visitors entering the Keeneland Amphitheater, Sandy was struck again by its beauty. It was like a theater-in-the-round, except the stage was square and covered with grass-green sawdust. Instead of a wooden rail separating the horses from the buyers a rope of white satin kept them apart. The effect was like a wedding; or maybe it was indeed a wedding, of a different sort.

The horses strutted by, sleek and bare except for a tiny white patch on their hips bearing a buy-number. All around, Sandy heard catalog pages rustling as the auctioneer's mellow voice called out each yearling's name and number with a quick description of its forebears.

In two hours she had bid on four yearlings, won three, and had made shipping arrangements. Then with a sudden need to get home she hailed a cab driver who could have been a graduate of the Indianapolis 500. His heavy foot and delicate hands helped her catch an earlier flight than the one she had planned to take. It set her down in Ocala before dusk.

When she turned her key in the front door she sensed that the house was deserted. "Judy! Pam! Chris!" she shouted. "Where is everybody?" The kitchen was quietest of all—with no pots bubbling on the stove, no familiar scents of onion and garlic and oregano, and no pit bull pup (Chris's latest pet) tumbling in circles at her feet.

Looking for a snack, she turned toward the cutting block and caught her breath at sight of a bud vase holding one yellow rose with a matching yellow note:

I'm a filly!
Mom and I are fine.
I'm pretty, too.

Sandy dropped everything. With her heart pounding she ran to Sunshine's paddock. In the dusky half-light a small chestnut face with a white blaze peered at her from around Sunshine's hindquarters.

At the sound of Sandy's voice Sunshine bolted toward her with an "I'm hungry" nicker. Slowly Sandy opened the gate, and to her delight and amazement, out jumped Sunshine's baby!

The foal was big and splashy with paint spots like Sunshine's, but with more white on her body. She had a lovely, balanced head and neck. Her legs were straight and she had a good shoulder and rump. She appeared to be perfect! As if to say, "I can move just fine, too—watch me," she gave a little buck and ran around Sunshine.

"Twilight," Sandy murmured. *Twilight!* What a blessed time of day for a blessed event! Instinctively Sandy had named the foal—not just because she first saw her in the mystic hour between sunset and dark night, but also because the foal was born in the twilight of Misty's era.

There are some moments that grownups just can't describe, but children can. Pam and Chris burst in on Sandy's joy.

"Mom!" they shouted in unison. "Mr. O'Quinn wasn't home. We ran to tell him about Sunshine's baby."

"Mom, you should have seen it," Pam said. "It was awesome."

"What was?"

"We found both Sunshine and her baby down."

"Yeah, they were both lying down . . ." Chris was quick to corroborate.

"But not all the way," Pam added. "Their front feet were set deep in the straw, but their necks and heads were up."

"What," Sandy asked, "is so awesome about that?"

"They were nose to nose."

Sandy's eyebrows shot up.

"Yes! They were! It was like they were saying, 'Who are you? And who are *you?*'"

Now Pam came over and reached for her mother's hand. Her voice was no longer loud and excited. In a whisper she confided, "Mom, it really was awesome. The baby was still wearing her sac, the one she lived in while she was inside Sunshine."

Sandy felt shivers in the small of her back. "But, Pam," she asked, "how could they have been nose to nose with the baby still wearing that strong sac?"

"Robert told us that in cleaning up her newborn, Sunshine must've pushed the sac to her shoulders before Robert got there. Robert was so funny. He just stood there, gawking and saying, 'Well, I'll be danged . . . she looks like a little old grand dame wearing a silk cape.'"

Chapter 10
WHY NOT?

Only in her golden-brown splashes of color and in her two-toned tail—half white, half brown—did Twilight resemble Sunshine. In her action and disposition she was as different as war from peace. Sunshine long ago had been gentled and had a tranquil nature; but it was the *hot* blood of Bold Ruler that had also been transmitted to Twilight.

Twilight was as unpredictable as a dangling electric wire. She liked to race along the fence rail, taunting the thoroughbreds on the other side, daring them to race. She had speed without question. She scared Sunshine and Sandy half to death as she skidded to the fence corners by sliding

on her haunches and waiting until the last second to wheel out. Her poor mother tried to follow with frustrated whinnies, but she just couldn't keep pace. None of the other Chincoteague ponies could. There was nothing tagalong about Twilight. She went far afield and returned only to nurse.

Unlike her mother, Twilight barely tolerated the bristles of the grooming brush and would pull away from a hand that longed to pet her. But in her frequent gallops she obviously enjoyed the cool fingers of the wind combing her coat.

Because Twilight was born at the wrong time of the year—in September instead of spring, when most of her thoroughbred neighbors were born—she had no foals to play with. Sunshine was the scapegoat for all of Twi's giddy antics. More than once, Robert caught her taking a quick nip at Sunshine's rump, then whirling around with a "catch-me-if-you-can" dare.

"Beats me," he laughed, "who's in control here. Seems Twilight makes up the rules, nip by nip."

When Twi outgrew milk and pellets and began chewing wisps of hay, Sunshine in no way objected. But when she began nosing into her mother's oats, mother and daughter had to be separated at mealtime. From then on Twi weaned herself.

Sandy refused to let Twilight be trained as early as

most thoroughbreds. She had seen many two-year-olds break down from racing before their bones were fully formed. Such a fate would not happen to Twilight. For two whole years they let Twilight run free in the pasture with her more placid Chincoteague friends.

Her only separation from them was a short confinement to a stall to await the farrier's examination of her feet. Most ponies would adjust to temporary restriction. Not Twilight! She could do more shenanigans in a twelve-by-twelve stall than most animals in an open pasture. She'd race. She'd rear. She'd buck herself into a lather. Then tensing every muscle, she'd crouch low and suddenly catapult herself straight up into the air . . . Once she bent an eight-foot steel door at the top while giving a last defiant kick.

In the quiet of her pasture, though, Twilight began training herself. This was her arena, and she made full use of it, clearing imaginary obstacles as if they'd been precisely laid out by a show committee.

Watching, the children and Sandy cheered her on, taking the jumps with her. Depending on how high or wide she'd jump, they'd shout,

"Over the chicken coop!"

"Over the post and rail."

"Oh no! Lookit! She just cleared a double-oxer."

The more horseplay she practiced, the more they

puzzled about her future. How should her strong competitive spirit be directed?

It was a scruffy, bumptious hound dog that provided the first answer. One autumn morning when the dew was still fresh, this stray hound, intent on sniffing the zigzag tracks of a rabbit, invaded Twilight's territory. Twi lifted her head from grazing and cast a baleful eye in the hound's direction. Her whole body cried out, "Let me at him!" Her ears pricked, her nostrils flared, her tail arched. For a moment she froze as if to plan a course of action. This *could* have given the hound time to retreat, but he only nosed deeper onto Twilight's territory.

The skirmish was on! Dirt flew from all four feet as Twi dug into the ground. Her ears flattened. Her neck stretched down to earth, and her jaws opened as she snaked after the enemy in a cutting position. She overtook him and began maneuvering him, twisting, turning him off his course, toward the fence line. For a full second the two creatures faced each other. Then the hound bolted toward the fence.

With the speed of light Twi intercepted him and tossed him up and over the top rail. The little fellow wasn't hurt, but he slunk away, never to return. Twilight trumpeted her victory to the skies. "That took care of him!" she said, plainer than if she had talked.

It was Twilight's lightning moves that triggered an

exciting idea. Sandy talked it over with her two young advisors. "Remember the cutting competition on 'The Wide World of Sports' where the famous horse, Cutter Bill, separated a cow out of a herd and penned it without even wearing a bridle?"

Chris waved his arms. "'Course I do! That horse went so fast, his hind legs whipped in one direction and his forelegs were following the cow in another."

Pam looked thoughtful. "Shucks, Mom, Twilight can do that."

Even with Pam's assurance Sandy came down to earth, suddenly remembering that Cutter Bill was a big quarter horse, *not* a Chincoteague pony!

She squelched the negative thought. Twi did seem to know all the right moves. What a challenge! What if she didn't have quarter horse blood? Her Chincoteague ancestors gave her grit and savvy. Added to her thoroughbred fire, she had it all. If she could outsmart a lightning-fast hunting hound, why not a big old cow? Or even a Brahman bull?

Why not?

Chapter 11
GENTLIN'?

A cutting horse is one of the fastest horses in the world for a quarter of a mile. He chases wild cattle, singles one out of a herd, and drives it into the cow pen.

Poor Twilight had never seen a cow, though. How could anyone expect her to perform the double miracle of speed and savvy?

"Let's not hurry her," Sandy said.

Each member of the family and farm agreed that the training of Twi had to go forward gradually. They were all aware of Twi's independence and her free spirit. "Our first step," Andrew reminded, "is to get her used to the lead rope."

Young Twilight did not fall in with the plan; she had

ideas of her own. What a fight she gave when first she felt the restriction of the rope!

The experience challenged horse and human. Twi taught the power of patience; she could not be forced into a new pattern. She learned, by dint of tolerance and much praise, that the rope was not a fearsome enemy at all—it was a helping device to lead her over logs and up and down ramps. Being of a curious nature she quickly made the connection that the rope opened new vistas . . . new sights and sounds and small animals to stare down.

Overcoming this first challenge convinced Sandy that with a knowledgeable trainer, Twilight could become a cutting horse to compete with the best. All Twi needed was expert breaking, or as Grandpa Beebe would have said, "extry gentlin'."

So with Andrew's approval, Sandy and Robert vanned Twilight to a pinto-horse trainer who had a good reputation. The man's assessment of Twilight's ability was quick and sure. "She moves well," he said, "and appears very alert. Come back in three weeks and she'll be ready to go home."

With crossed fingers they left Twi behind. She was so young and free from restraints and filled with such enthusiasm for life. Sandy could only hope they'd chosen the best way to shape and direct that fire.

For Sandy the twenty-one days of waiting dragged

heavily. She tried to fill the time with work and routine, but nothing seemed to make the hours pass any quicker.

Finally, the scheduled morning for pickup arrived. Sandy awoke to a dreary downpour, but found herself singing, "Oh, what a beau-ti-ful morning . . ." despite the weather.

She and Robert left early with the trailer all spic and span, not forgetting a small bag of Red Pippin apples, juicy and fragrant. When they arrived at the little farm, a stablehand stood in the vicinity of Twilight's stall and waved them on. Sandy smiled in anticipation as she hurried to Twi's open door.

One glance inside, and red-hot blood rushed to Sandy's throat. Who was this nervous, ribbed creature? How could Twilight have lost that much weight in only three weeks? She was cross tied, to be ready for departure perhaps, but if there was one restriction Twi couldn't abide, this was it.

Sandy glanced at Robert. His lips were pressed tight, and he had the stance of a fighter, his rope coiled in one hand and the other clenched at the ready. "Likely she's dropped fifty pounds!" He spat the words. "Where's that dirty so-and-so? I'll show him what I think of his training."

The stablehand left on the double. "I'll get your trainer," he called over his shoulder.

"If it would help Twilight, I'd join the fight," Sandy

said, "but the damage is done. Let's just get her out of here. And fast."

At the sound of Sandy's voice, Twilight began to tremble. Sandy found herself trembling, too.

The trainer, looking very innocent, came swaggering up to them. He tried to placate Sandy. "I'm happy to say, Doc Price, your pony is well broken."

The word "broken" cut like a knife.

In a conciliatory tone he added, "She'll make a good English pleasure horse. Her only problem is not wanting to stop in a gallop."

"An English pleasure horse that won't stop? That adds insult to injury." Sandy sputtered in frustration. She went to Twi and put both her hands on her horse's sweating body. "You can count on me to fix your good reputation," she said to the trainer. "I only hope we can rescue Twi from your abusive and unfeeling treatment."

Robert, twice the size of the trainer, used his arm as a broom and brushed the man aside. With lightning fingers he undid the cross tie and fastened his lead rope to Twi's halter. With a surge of new life, Twi snorted her relief and staggered into the trailer.

Twi came home to a warrior's welcome. Carrots and kisses from the children, supplemental nutrients from Robert, and a slow resumption of her home training.

The last straw of shame for Twi's ex-trainer was still to be reckoned with. One day when Sandy was examining Twilight's teeth to see if they needed rasping, she discovered to her horror that Twi's tongue had a deep cut across it.

It was put there, she assumed, to make Twi more sensitive to the pull of the bit. That hateful trainer had done it again! Sandy wanted to scream, but no sound came. It would take weeks for Twi to learn all over again to trust those who had sent her away.

While waiting for Twilight to heal, Sandy made the decision to register her in the Paint Horse Association. But with a quick refusal, the Association promptly turned Twi down. "That Chincoteague pony blood is her downfall," they said.

"Ironic," Sandy told the registrar, "because Arabians, thoroughbreds, and paint ponies all originated from prestigious Spanish bloodlines just as the Chincoteague ponies did."

Sandy was in no way intimidated. Next she tried the Pinto Horse Association of America and was delighted to learn that flashy color was the first requirement. Certainly Twi's bold patches would stand her in good stead. After color, the second requirement gave even deeper satisfaction. A single name such as Twilight was unacceptable.

There had to be a second name.

"I've got it! The perfect name!" Sandy cried. Tossing aside her ink-shy desk pen, she grabbed a bold magic marker and right in the middle of the application printed the words:

MISTY'S TWILIGHT

Chapter 12
THE CUTTING-HORSE MAN

Months later, when Twilight was once again her wild and shining self, Sandy received a telephone call from her friend, Kathy Daley, a young horsewoman who had shown Chris's Patches and Pam's Pie as yearlings. They hadn't won anything in three tries—not even a pink ribbon! The judges had ruled out the colts for not being registered.

"Sandy!" the familiar voice came over, young and strong. "I've found a trainer that you—and Twilight—must meet."

Sandy bristled. How could she subject Twilight to another grueling experience? She didn't answer.

Kathy's enthusiasm was undimmed.

"Sandy! At least you've got to meet the man. He's leasing stalls, taking on new students, and he lives close by."

"What's his name?"

"Richard Rank."

"Never heard of him."

"He's a cutting-horse man! I've seen him work."

Now Sandy was torn between curiosity and doubt. If there was anyone whose judgment she *could* trust, it was Kathy.

"Let me think it ov—"

Kathy interrupted, her words tumbling fast. "Sandy, please listen. Tonight at seven I'll be going right by Stolen Hours Farm. I'll stop by and pick you up, and you can meet the man, make up your own mind, and be back home in an hour. Bring Pam and Chris along; their instincts are good."

Sandy laughed. How could she refuse this good friend and marvelous horsewoman?

Two hours later Sandy, Chris, and Pam were hurrying down the driveway to meet Kathy. In less than half an hour's drive, the carful of cautious, yet excited pony people arrived at Rank's farm. There they saw six neat horse stalls next to a new eight-foot round pen that had been built for an arena. Brahman cattle grazed in the field beyond. An evening peace had settled over the land. Chores were done. Horses were looking out of their stalls, grinding twists of hay that wisped out from their mouths like handlebar mustaches.

Sandy shook hands with Mr. Richard Rank and promised herself to make haste slowly this time.

"Twilight has so much to learn," she explained to him. "She's never even seen a cow up close, let along a Brahman bull. You wouldn't start her off with the Brahmans, would you?"

Dick Rank raised his eyebrows. "Why not?"

"Because their horns scare me half to death! I've seen them gore a horse!"

The man didn't laugh. "I have, too," he admitted, "but Brahmans are good performers. They actually challenge the horse to give chase; they give the beginner an opportunity to learn."

He smiled. "Your friend Kathy here has told me about Twilight's spit and spunk and her wild background; and her gentleness, too. That's the kind of information I need. And I hope you'll all call me Dick," he added with a grin. "My kids tell me 'Rank' is too smelly a name."

Without being asked Chris announced, "I think Rank's a smelly name, too. The man's okay, Mom. He looks me right in the eye. Let's go with Dick."

Within an hour's time, Dick, the children, and Sandy had come to an agreement, and Kathy, humming at the wheel, was driving them home.

Before bedtime, Sandy slipped out to be with Twilight, to tell her, "I think we are *finally* on our way!" She let Twi lip her hair while reveling in the thought that now, during *this* training, she could and would visit often . . .

Sandy meant to give Dick a week's testing before she went over to see what he had accomplished. Truth is, she and Pam and Chris went visiting after only two days.

When they arrived, there was Twi, bucking and kicking the walls of her stall, eager to break loose. They retreated to a viewpoint outside the arena to watch Dick's first ride. Dick led the prancing Twilight into the arena and swung aboard.

At that, Twi stood on her hind legs and pawed the air. She reared and bucked and kicked as if she were a rodeo pony. Why, she jumped so high all four feet were three feet in the air! Dick held on.

The kids clapped and cheered. "She's great, Mom!"

Then, with one final kick Dick was on the ground and Twi was free once again. She had won the first skirmish after all.

The second visit, three days later, proved wholly different, but just as exciting. From their assigned vantage point outside the arena the kids and Sandy held their breath to watch Dick and his helper clip Twi's coat for summer. As soon as Dick turned on the razor, Twi was alerted and leaned into the shiny instrument. Obviously

she enjoyed the vibration to her ribs, but when the buzzing thing climbed up her neck close to her ear, she exploded. She broke loose from the twitch and from the two men, but got her ear nipped in the process. Eyes blazing, she crouched, ready to spring at anyone who made a move.

Dick took off his hat and laughed. "Her message is clear. You dare come closer and I'll get you!"

Sandy joined in the laughter. more from nerves than from finding anything funny about the situation. Then Dick said, "I like this horse's spirit. Spitfires often make the best cutting horses."

Before the kids and Sandy left that day, Twi was back in her stall and rubbing an itchy place on her shoulder against Dick's back as he cut a salt block in half for her to lick.

As they drove home Sandy had the distinct feeling that Misty's Twilight was destined to electrify the cutting-horse world.

Chapter 13
DREAM ON, LADY

The story of the cutting horse has not been fully told. What a loss to those who have not seen him work! Intelligence, courage, anticipation, patience, control, tenacity, athletic ability—all are required. Originally he was bred for work, not show. Cattlemen needed a horse of immense power and flexibility—one that could brace himself against the shock of a thousand pounds of wild steer at the end of a rope, and, in the next instant, snake through a herd to single out just the calf his rider is after. The horse took over where man's prompting stopped. Man had told him *what* he wanted, *where* he wanted it, and *when* to let go. After that the horse was on his own, his job to outthink and outmaneuver the calf or steer.

Anyone who has ever seen a cutting match realizes that once the chase is on, the rider is more or less a non-interfering passenger, holding onto the saddle horn, if necessary.

The cutting horse still works on great cattle ranches, but often the owner becomes so proud of his favorite "cutter" that he enters him in shows against the bigger, tougher, more experienced quarter horses.

Could Twi, the Chincoteague pony, become a cutter?

It was clear that she enjoyed her training days with Dick. She learned to listen for his voice commands and react instantly. Daily her technique improved—balancing on her haunches, spinning, dashing, dancing at the cow's whim. She learned to "catwalk" into a herd of cattle and concentrate on one cow's moves. Without the slightest hesitation she could "cut the critter out" and keep her out.

"It's sheer hypnosis!" Dick pronounced.

Other owners often flocked around Twilight after her training session. Some were astride, some with horse in hand, some afoot, but each fired questions in quick succession.

"Who's the pinto?" was always first.

Dick answered with a show of pride. "Her registry," he said, "is Misty's Twilight. But we call her Twi."

"Never heard of her. What's she doing here?"

"She's learning to compete with the quarter horses."

"What's her breed?"

Whenever Sandy was on hand, Dick nodded in her direction. "Ask her doctor-owner," he'd say.

Sandy, taking a deep breath, would summon all of her patience. "Her breeding," she'd say in her most professional tone, "is Chin-co-teague," and she'd stretch out each syllable until it snapped like a rubber band.

"Hmm. That's nice! *But what in tunket is Jinkatig?* I've never heard of that horse."

When the questions were asked in genuine interest, Sandy would offer to lend a copy of *Misty of Chincoteague.* Sometimes, though, the questions were tossed out like a fighting glove. Then Sandy would take up the gauntlet and the explanations would last belligerently all morning long.

One day a big-bellied snipe of a man taunted: "Lady, your pinto's a pretty little thing, but don't expect her to compete with our brainy quarter horses."

Sandy blurted out her intentions angrily. "We plan on taking her right to the top!"

The little man on the big horse laughed. As he turned to leave, he tossed a final twit over his shoulder. *"Dream on, lady."*

When the day arrived for Twilight's first competition—at the State Fair in Tampa, Florida—she traveled well.

Once at the fair, though, her mind was on tiptoe. Instead of remembering Dick's training, she was distracted by the new sights, sounds, and smells of the fair grounds—the people, children, dogs, horses. One stallion especially piqued her interest. She tossed her head and let out a string of high whinnies. She was nervous, and she was curious. Cows were fine most of the time, but stallions, now—they were new and exciting.

Twi's first real chance to prove herself a cutter was a disaster! When it was her turn to compete, she lined up

behind the starting rope just as she was supposed to, but instead of facing forward to challenge her quarry, her head turned every which-a-way, distracted by everything. As a result, she got a slow start and her forelegs gave only a weak push-off. She lagged behind—split seconds only— but those seconds were enough to keep her from scoring any points. What a learning experience!

Back to work. In no way disappointed, Dick repeated the test training until Twi moved her head and neck freely in response to the movements of the chosen calf. Almost simultaneously Twi put on that strutting action with her forelegs to make a quick stop. The startled calf put on his brakes, too.

Dick worked with Twi all summer long, grinning his approval. When she hunkered down low, to face a calf full on, she was only two strides away, blocking it from rejoining the herd. Dick encouraged Twi's every move.

Neighbor kids hanging on the fence rails rooted for the calf. They cheered in defense of Twi's actions while the immobile passenger, deep in the saddle, yodeled Twi's name. She was working wholly on her own! She would not be penalized by *anything*. She was maneuvering her quarry, maneuvering the bull calf farther and farther from the herd.

Fall came on with golden days. Twi, with Dick aboard, went to three competitions in quick succession. And she began to win! Soon streamers with inch-thick red letters blazed above the magazine rack in Sandy's waiting room, advertising Twi's success:

MISTY'S TWILIGHT BORDERING ON FULL CHAMPIONSHIP IN PENNSYLVANIA

Then the bombshell! On the night of Twi's latest triumph a long distance call cleaved the darkness while the banner still fluttered in Dr. Sandy's office. She didn't recognize the voice on the phone; it was a telegram call from Dick. Without any explanation it said, *"Am sending Twi home."*

Before Sandy could ask a question, the phone went dead and a busybody mechanical voice said: *"If you'd like to make a call, please hang up and dial again."*

Chapter 14
HOME AGAIN

Mornings with dew on the grass and Chincoteague colts rolling in sand and sun—this was Stolen Hours—each hour precious. And Twi was back!

Not everyone accepted her at first. "This is *our* territory—who is this interloper?" Patches, Pie, and Piper all seemed to say. Even Sunshine eyed her own daughter with misgiving.

For Sandy, having Twilight on the farm again would have been an unmixed blessing, if only she had some explanation from Dick Rank as to why he had sent Twi home. But the only excuses he ever gave her were unsatisfactory ones, and after awhile she stopped trying to guess at the real reasons. The new task that occupied her mind was figuring out what Twilight's next challenge was to be.

Twi had her own time adjusting to a life of leisure. For a while she went back to running along the fence lines as if she were continuing her training. Skidding to a stop at the corners, spinning on her haunches like a true cutting horse, and racing back again was her only preoccupation in life. It seemed she had spent so much time training and competing, she had forgotten how to play. Idleness, routine, and scenery were not enough for her. But gradually the tranquility of the farm seemed to take hold of her. Scattered woods with oak and sweet gum, hickory, dogwood, and pine trees were there for exploring, as though for the first time. Even the pond was peaceful and soothing. Twi drank and then rolled in the long grass. At last she slept, and quiet returned to Stolen Hours Farm.

The Chincoteaque ponies seemed to settle down, too. They must have realized that Twi was not a stranger after all.

Just as Sandy, Pam, and Chris went back to their normal daily routines, a real stranger came all the way from England to inspect Stolen Hours.

His name was Mr. Derek Sutton, and he was a dignified English gentleman who had become somewhat portly with age. He was now a retired thoroughbred trainer and steeplechase rider gone out to pasture with his horses.

Actually, he had come to the United States with the hope of moving his family to Florida to see if this kind of life would suit him and his elderly gelding.

Andrew, who also hailed from England, treated the Englishman with respect, allowing him to roam at will. Sandy returned from her office one evening, and was surprised but gracious when she found an Englishman playing with their rottweiler hound and looking fully relaxed and at home.

After a few pleasantries, Sutton said, "Your man gave me free rein to take an overall look at Stolen Hours."

Sandy smiled. "He has that privilege," she said.

"Would you have any objection to my setting up a beginning cross-country jump course through your woods? You see, Dr. Price, I'm stabling my elderly gelding at the small inn where I'm staying. He's in need of exercise, and so am I!"

Sandy thought for a moment. "This might be just the thing for Twi." Out loud she said, "Yes, of course you may, on condition that you'll try our pinto, Twilight, along with your gelding."

Sutton was not enthusiastic, but he did manage to mumble, "Harumph, I'll give it a go."

To his surprise and Sandy's delight, Twilight jumped the pond and low logs with ease. She'd be perfectly at home on a beginning course.

"Hmm," said Sutton, shaking his head. "You know, of course, that it would take years of training for her to negotiate the big jumps. . . ."

Sandy jumped in, as he hesitated. "What would be her limitations?"

"The biggest drawback," he said, biting off each word, "is her size. She's too small to carry a big man like me and still have enough power to clear the jumps. And then there's her color, of course. It doesn't help. I call it more clownlike than regal." With these words Sutton refused the conditions. Then with a tip of his hat he went on his way to investigate other possibilities.

Chapter 15
NEVER?

Once again, Sandy was left wondering what to choose for Twilight's future. Like a cat, she could have nine lives. She could be an endurance horse, race horse, calf-roping or barrel-racing horse, harness horse, hunter or jumping horse—or a three-day-event horse, the decathlete of the equestrian world!

Or, Sandy told herself, Twi could finish what she'd already begun.

"It's hard finding the right slot for her," Clayton O'Quinn told Sandy one day. "Twilight is not an easy horse to classify."

"I know," Sandy said. "She's one of a kind, and I love

her for that. It's part of what makes her great. You know, in the far-off future, I don't rule out the Olympics."

"Begorry!" O'Quinn lapsed into his Irishness. "You dream big, Sandy. But the question is, what will she do *now*?"

"For now, Clayton, maybe she should complete her cutting chapter," Sandy said quietly.

"I was thinking the very same thought, even though the girl at the Pinto Horse Association told me that a pinto's action has to be twice as sure as any other horse's for the judge to even look at it. She says there's never been a pinto cutting horse that was a winner."

"Never?" Sandy smiled. "What a fickle word!"

Fate plays a big role in our lives. It must have been fate that prompted Sandy to pick up a horse magazine, one day soon after her conversation with O'Quinn, and turn to an article about a cutting-horse trainer from Dothan, Alabama. His name was Buddy Tate and he was scheduled to judge a show right near Ocala on Wednesday next. He was touted as one of the most knowledgeable cutting-horse trainers.

Before Sandy could forget the spelling of Dothan, she pulled out her road map and traced the route from Apalachee Bay, on up the Chattachoochee River to Dothan. Then with red ink she circled the date of the

Florida show on her calendar. Over the black numerals she wrote *Twilight's future?*

On Wednesday afternoon Sandy could hardly wait to say good-bye to her last patient. A short time later she was rubbing elbows with owners and horse people of all ages and sizes. She watched two pintos in the competition, but neither won so much as a pink ribbon. "Could it really be true that a pinto's color works against him?" she asked herself.

After the show was over, Sandy joined the long line of folks wanting to meet Judge Buddy Tate. He looked tired, as if he wanted to bolt for home, but he blotted his brow and managed a smile when it finally came Sandy's turn. That was all the encouragement she needed.

"Our Twilight is a tornado, even if she is wearing clown's colors," she announced without any other opening. "And she's ready to show her stuff."

Judge Tate glanced at his watch. "You live near here?" was the only thing he asked.

"About thirty minutes away," Sandy replied breathlessly.

"Okay. Lead the way."

At Stolen Hours, Chris and Pam had just finished sloshing water over Twilight. They earned part of their allowance by grooming the horses after school. The day had turned hot and muggy, and Twi was enjoying her bath without any of her usual fidgeting.

A rub-rag still in his hand, Robert hastened to meet Sandy and the judge as they got out of their cars. When Sandy introduced him to Buddy Tate his eyes widened in awed respect.

"He's here to see Twilight," Sandy explained.

Robert swung into action. He snapped a lead rope to Twi's halter and began trotting her in an ever-widening circle. Twi was in her element. She tossed her mane, arched her tail, and pranced as if she were leading a parade.

Pam and Chris clapped noisily. Sandy gave them a shushing look, and all waited silently for Judge Tate's reaction.

The answer came with agonizing slowness. "Quarter horses take all the ribbons."

"Yes, I've noticed." Sandy wiped her sweating palms on her pants legs and waited for him to go on.

"She'll be soft after not working awhile."

"I know that, too."

Then he shook his head and gave a suppressed laugh, as if surprised at his own impulsiveness. "There's something about Twilight's spirit that impresses me. I believe I could put a happy ending to her story."

Sandy's heart bumped into her throat. The kids let out a cheer.

Three days later Twilight was shipped to Dothan, Alabama. The lively way she hightailed it into the van without urging was proof enough that travel and adventure were her lifestyle.

Chapter 16
JUDGE TATE

Almost before Twilight had time to settle in, Sandy was on her way to Dothan. She missed the spunky mare that much. When she arrived, trainer Tate was riding Twi around and around in the big open pen.

It was clear that he was enjoying Twilight's free-flowing trot and hated to stop. But when he did he was eager to talk.

"Doctor Sandy," he said, patting Twi's shoulder as he rode over to greet her, "I'm delighted with your one-of-a-kind pinto! She has a class and style all her own."

Sandy grinned like a proud parent.

"And she's so fresh," Buddy Tate went on. "She isn't

burned out at all. How do you account for that?"

Twilight began whuffing Sandy's hand. Her warm breath smelled grassy and good. Sandy smiled at the ticklish feeling.

"For the first two years of Twi's life," she explained, "she ran wild and free on Stolen Hours Farm, the way her forebears did on Assateague Island."

"That's it!" Tate exclaimed. "No pushing and training as a colt. I've seen many a burned-out two-year-old. Fact is I saw a pretty little filly shot dead at the track because of a broken leg too shattered for splints."

Sandy shuddered. She had heard of the same thing. "What a horrifying waste of a young horse's life. Sometimes, Mr. Tate, I think we people are pretty heartless about the wild things who share our world."

Nodding, Buddy Tate loosened Twi's girth strap and then laid her saddle over the fence rail. He hung her bridle on the post and turned her loose with an affectionate pat. Sandy watched as Twi tossed her head and sucked in great draughts of morning air.

"I have a story to tell you, Doc," Tate said, breaking in on Sandy's thoughts. "The other day, Twi out-and-out asked me to be her pal and protector."

"How do you mean?" Sandy turned to him, eager to hear the story.

"It was during a blast of winter wind," he told her,

"that I stapled plastic over the outside windows of the stalls around the working arena. As the storm heightened, the plastic began to flap and crackle. I tell you, it was like hearing the cracking bones of some fierce demon! Anyway, Twi went into a wingding. I told her she'd have to get used to it.

"Now, Doc, get this. Your big brave tornado of a pony turned into a skittery kitten. She followed me around the arena, not letting me get more'n two feet away from her. I could see the fear in her eyes, she was that terrified. And then came the sound of one of the Brahmans, lowing over the storm.

"At that, Twilight's whole body trembled with the question. It was as if she were saying to me, 'You don't expect me to work the cows by myself, do you? Please stay close. We'll face those big-eared critters together.'"

Sandy burst out laughing. "Why, I can hardly believe it," she said. "Twi always seems so fearless."

"Well, now you know she's normal. And she still has a lot to learn about cutting. But I will tell you this. Where she really excels is in her people sense."

"How did you discover that?"

"One day my little girl begged to ride Twi," Tate explained. "She had just mucked out three stalls, and this was the only reward she wanted. While I nervously

watched, your pony was as gentle as a lamb. She knew just what to do and when."

Sandy nodded. "That's Twilight all over!"

Five weeks into her training Twilight went to her first big cutting show, in Montgomery, Alabama. She had only won the 500-level novice before, with Dick Rank as her trainer, but now Buddy Tate selected the 1500 for her first professional start. She placed second!

Twi quickly progressed to the 3000-level classes, then to the 5000—each time performing harder tasks, and each time winning. She learned to work without a bridle, just as the great horse Cutter Bill had done on television. It seemed she was well on her way.

Then fate stepped in again, and the pendulum that seemed to rule Twi's life swung back from its giddy height. The owner of Buddy's farm died suddenly, and Buddy and his family had to look for a new location. They found a suitable place near Stolen Hours Farm in Ocala, and with Sandy's help, Buddy was soon in business again. But things were a little different in Florida than they had been in Alabama.

In her new surroundings Twilight shone. She thought and reacted more quickly than many people. If a calf just stood there bawling, Twi snaked directly toward her until the lazy thing went into combat. "That," Buddy bragged, "is how Twi demonstrates her intelligence."

It was also how she stirred up the competition. Owners of big, brawny quarter horses soon became very curious about this upstart in their midst.

One day when Sandy was walking Twilight to cool her down, a swaggering cowpuncher stopped her. "You own that paint, don't you, lady?"

Sandy nodded.

"What in the world kind of breed is *that*?" he drawled.

"Chincoteague, of course," Sandy said. "With a pinch of thoroughbred."

"Where does she get her cow savvy?" he asked with a pained expression. "Certainly not from *that* combination."

Sandy laughed, though in truth she felt as though Twi was being insulted. "Why not? She inherited the best of both."

The man shrugged, muttering to himself, "Painted horses and lady owners shouldn't be allowed."

As time went by, it became clear that the quarter horse owners resented Twi's flair for the spectacular. They found her cleverness hard to tolerate. They began not to accept her at the higher levels of competition. "Where would we class her?" they asked. "She just doesn't fit in anywhere."

Sandy's friend Clayton O'Quinn analyzed the situation

with his special wisdom. "It's like this, Sandy," he said. "Twi just isn't built like the average cutting horse. She's delicate and pretty. When she crosses the arena using that paradelike trot of hers, people think she won't be able to cut out the calves. And when she does it, they think she's a freak horse."

Sandy swallowed bitter disappointment. Twilight's spotted coat didn't help. Her high spirits didn't help. Her natural horse and cow sense didn't help. And to top it all off, here in Florida, the Alabama trainer, Buddy Tate, was a rank outsider. The fact that he worked with a prize pinto pony like Twi was making his life difficult, too.

And so the odds won out. When Sandy asked Buddy to show Twilight one more time, he declined with an embarrassed look on his face. "I'm afraid my trailer's full already," he explained.

Again, a cold wind blew in Sandy's face. Perhaps that was why Dick Rank had stopped working with Twi; maybe he'd had the same trouble with the prejudice against pintos.

But she refused to be daunted for long. "If Twi's cutting career isn't going to work," she said to her farm manager, Andrew, "we'll move on to plan B!"

"Plan B?" Andrew asked with a lift of his eyebrows.

"That's right. Your countryman, Mr. Derek Sutton, seemed to think Twilight was too small and funny-looking to make a world-class jumper. Well, I intend to prove him wrong."

"All right, Doc," Andrew said. "Whatever you decide to do, I'm with you."

"It's all such silly prejudice," Sandy fumed. "What does color have to do with jumping? For that matter, what does size have to do with it? With her long strides, Twi will make it over the triple jumps with ease."

"Especially with a woman aboard," Andrew agreed.

Sandy felt the old thrill of excitement. *"And that woman could be me."*

Chapter 17

KRITTER KORNER

Andrew and Sandy were quick to lay out a course through the woods to test Twi's limits. First they piled up two logs, then three, and then around the bend another makeshift triple. The pond, of course, was a natural water jump and the gate that opened onto the show ring could easily serve as the high point.

Twi and Sandy both seemed happiest when at work, and work it was. First Sandy carefully walked Twi around the course so she could see what she was up against. Then Andrew tried Twi out, one jump at a time. Twi's training, in stopping and starting, quickly stood her in good stead. One quick glance at the upcoming obstacle and she was ready for takeoff, needing only heels and knees to guide her.

Twi was in her element. The higher the jump, the better she liked it. Tossing and snorting she cavorted around the course as though she owned it. And, in fact, she did. Soon Andrew was just the passenger and Sandy the spellbound observer.

Then, wham! The teeter-totter of Twi's way of life took over once again. Just as Sandy was thinking that Twi was ready to compete as a jumper, she noticed a slight swelling of Twi's left foreankle. She called a vet immediately. The diagnosis was grim.

"I can't believe," the vet said, "that your mare is moving sound. The X ray shows an old fracture of the sesamoid bone. It will be okay to ride her, but too risky to push her into any serious jumping events. I'm so sorry."

Poor Twi! Sandy felt sure that Twi was puzzled and wondering what had happened to spoil her fun. She clearly loved cross-country jumping.

Sandy sought a second opinion. The second vet ordered a farrier to put a set of pads on Twi's feet to cushion the strain of walking, trotting, and cantering on that left foreleg. And he, too, warned, *"No jumping!"*

The pads were meant to last six months; Twi wore them out in six weeks! Then she began frisking about in

relief. A mare with less heart might have favored that left foreleg, but not Twi. As the months went by she kept testing it, kept using it, and then began her old nervous pacing for want of something to do. In her highest bugle, she announced to the world that she was eager and ready to go to work.

During this lull in Twi's life. Sandy's old friend and horsewoman came to visit at Stolen Hours. Kathy Daley and Sandy had known each other from the time Kathy was six years old, a spunky kid in her first show! And now she was a trainer at a place called Kritter Korner, where horses of all ages were revitalized.

Sandy and Kathy talked about Twi's history and her ups and downs. Why were there so many downs? Sandy wanted to know.

There was no despair about Kathy. She was not the least depressed. Fact was, she bubbled with plans. "Sandy," she said with a spark in her eye, "if it can't be cutting or jumping for Twi, why not dressage? Twi's such a natural performer, and so obedient to her riders. She's much too competitive to be confined to pasture the rest of her life. Let me take her to Kritter Korner and see what we can do."

Sandy caught Kathy's enthusiasm and laughed. "Yes, let's do it! I can already see Twi up on her toes, dancing to the music of the Blue Danube waltz." She grabbed

Kathy's hands and they whirled around the kitchen, bouncing once again in anticipation of things to come.

The day that Twilight moved in—saddle and bridle, hoof pick and tail comb—her reception at Kritter Korner was like a rowdy high-school reunion. The noise was a merry mishmash of sounds. Snortings and squealings, brayings and buglings. Twi was the celebrity of the day.

She was responded with joyful bucks and nips, punctuated by her curious whinnies. From frisky young critters to trembly-lipped old-timers, Twilight had been accepted!

Almost before Twi had a chance to settle in, the training began. Kathy was delighted with this one-of-a-kind pinto with a class and a style all her own. Far from wearing her out, the hardships seemed only to make Twi stronger, fresher, more eager to please and perform. The wild freedom of her Assateague forebears and her early years at Stolen Hours Farm kept her from being burned out too soon.

Early one morning, Kathy turned Twi loose with an affectionate slap on the rump. She watched Twi toss her head. For a split second, she galvanized herself, then sprang into the air in an almost perfect *Capriole*, as stately as any Lipizzaner of Vienna. She kicked out with such force that all four legs went flying as if she was determined to separate herself from herself.

Kathy called Sandy at her office. "I guess there isn't anything our Twi can't do!"

Chapter 18
THE NIGHT OF THE VCR

From her toes to the top of her ponytail, Kathy stood only fifteen hands high. What a neat happenstance! This made Twilight appear as stately as the revered Lipizzaners, the ballet dancers of the horse world.

Like a good "parent" Sandy stayed away from Twi's schooling to give Kathy free rein. But what a long year it was! Pam had started college and Chris was away at boarding school. His teenage mischief-making was someone else's concern now. Pie, Patches, Piper, and Sunshine seemed lost without the children and Sandy was lost without Twilight. Daytimes Sandy was so busy studying her patients' problems that she didn't think about the quiet at

110

home. But at dusk, after work, the relative silence struck her hard. No high-pitched whinnying. No kids home from school.

For escape and companionship Sandy took Chris's big Rhodesian pit bull and two suppers—usually dog munchies for Rhodi and peanut-butter sandwiches for herself—to the comfort of her bedroom where she listened to music . . . anything from classical to rock. The day's mail had already been piled up on her bed with a trash basket nearby.

One late evening, while throwing away the junk mail, Sandy's eyes caught a slim box marked "Video—Handle With Care." The return address read *Kritter Korner*. She brushed the other mail aside and with quick fingers tore open the wrapping and slid the cassette into her VCR.

Instantly Sandy was on the floor with Rhodi—an audience of two sitting on the floor, watching an elegant pinto pony going through difficult dressage movements. Of course it was Twilight. It had to be! Her sparkling white patches were all in the right places. But there was a strange new elegance about her—a presence, a nobility. The high head carriage, the arched neck, the feather step. Even at the collected walk, her hind legs were well under her body, her action elevated.

Kathy, too, had changed. She was the Hofrat, the riding master. She was up-headed, *too*, her back ramrod

straight. Yet she seemed utterly relaxed. Sandy was mesmerized. She heard her own voice saying, "How do you
do it? How can you give secret signals to Twi that nobody
can detect?" She stopped talking to herself and watched
Twilight do the half-pass, stepping diagonally forward on
her tiptoes, as if she had been born to dance.

Now pony and rider were cantering around the arena
in lilting rhythm, then back to the collected walk, then the
canter again, changing leads from the right forehoof to the
left, then back again, every fourth stride.

Sandy sighed in happiness. The weight and wait of all
those years lifted. Twi had found herself.

As Sandy stood up, a yellow note fell from her lap.

Dear Sandy,
Twi's progress has been as changeable as the weather, but
always moving forward . . . sometimes at a slow pace, sometimes
with fire and imagination.
I think she has enjoyed the months of learning, and my belief
in her has never flagged.
On Thursday, the 23rd, Twilight faces her first recognized
Dressage Training Show. She's ready. I hope you'll be there, too.
Love,
Kathy

"Oh! No!" Sandy wailed to Rhodi. "The twenty-third

is today!" To soothe her disappointment she played the tape a second time, then reluctantly crawled into bed. Sleep came, but it was shot through with a dream. Twi was in her first show, doing her passages and pirouettes so elegantly that she trounced all competitors. Then suddenly she gave a mighty swish with her two-toned tail and swept all the judges off their feet. Their scorecards flew into the air. In her dream, the spectators were noisy with cheers and laughter.

"Yeah, Pinto!
Right on, Pinto!
A-w r-i-g-h-t!"

Sandy's own voice woke her up, cheering and laughing with the crowd.

Next morning she took off for the library. She just had to learn the mysteries of dressage. How was the horse prompted? What were the signals for each movement—from the simple walk, trot, canter to the passage and the piaffe? A librarian proudly brought out a worn French book by Guérinière, dated 1733, and Sandy spent a magic hour learning the answers.

Twi needed no help from books. She understood Kathy's body language.

When Sandy arrived at her office later that morning, a stark note stared up at her.

KATHY FROM KRITTER KORNER CALLED. WILL CALL BACK.

Sandy didn't wait. She dialed Kathy's number and held her breath. Something dreadful must have happened for her to phone during office hours.

"Oh, Sandy!" The line went silent until a sob broke through with Kathy's incredible confession. "In the show yesterday," the words tumbled over each other, "Twi won a first and a second."

"Why, that's wonderful!" Sandy exclaimed.

"How can second place be wonderful? It was *my* fault. I took her off course. She should have won two firsts!"

"What a relief!" Sandy cried. "I thought something dreadful had happened to you or to Twi. In my mind I saw her lying on her side, with blood trickling from her nostrils, and your riding britches all covered with her blood."

"No! No! Nothing like that, you silly. But the second place was not Twi's error. It was *mine! I took her off course.*"

Sandy laughed outright, and Kathy's tone brightened . . . somewhat.

"I guess I shouldn't feel too guilty, because one of the judges called me aside at the end of the show to say she was amazed at Twi's early ability."

Now Kathy's voice went up the scale and her words spilled out like M&Ms from a bag. "There's more! The judge said that any trainers, owners, or showers who want to understand the secret of good dressage should bring their finest-tipped brushes to paint Twilight in action."

Chapter 19
WHISTLING IN THE RAIN

Being just an owner instead of a day-to-day trainer had its drawbacks. Sandy missed the cozy everyday intimacy of sharing an apple with Twi, bite for bite. And she missed the sound of a low whickering in response to her coded whistle. She longed to see how cleanly her beloved Twilight had leaped from the hell-bent-for-leather work of the cutting horse to the thrills of jumping, to the final exultation of the dressage artist.

After months without any contact Sandy had to find out if any bond between them still existed. She determined to learn if, in her new role, Twilight still remembered her.

Purposely she did not set a definite appointment with Kathy. She preferred to arrive unannounced, hoping to see Twi alone. Certainly she'd be out in the pasture; she would kick her stall to kindling, if she hadn't been turned out into the gentle December rain.

These thoughts skirmished in Sandy's mind as her need to see Twi became stronger and stronger. Twi used to love the smell of work clothes. Sandy had dressed carefully in her old, smelly riding boots and her well-worn coat and pants. She worried to herself: Will Twi recognize the smell of me? Will she remember my whistle?

As Sandy neared Kritter Korner she rolled down her car window. She licked her lips and took a deep breath to practice her whistle. All that escaped was a puny squeak. Where in the world had that sissy tremolo come from? It would never carry to the far end of the pasture where, of course, Twi would be, head low, letting the rain slosh over her body.

She swallowed hard and tried a second whistle. A weird sound came out, like a frog croaking in the rain. Her third attempt produced a loud penetrating whistle. A passing driver gave her a scoffing look and shook his fist. She closed her window and drove on, trying to comfort herself with the old bromide, "When a dress rehearsal is a flop, the real performance is a triumph."

• • •

Out in the pasture she saw a huddle of big horses with a pony in front center. All stood with their rumps to the wind. They were identical in color—wetted dark by the rain. The arrival of the car didn't disturb them. Not an ear swiveled.

Kathy was nowhere in sight. Sandy felt like an actor on an empty stage.

She leaned on the fence rail, oblivious to the wetness, and sucked in a great gulp of air. In a clear tone that she scarcely recognized as her own she steam-whistled her

two-note call. A faraway ear swiveled as if asking, "Eh? Will you please run that by me again?"

Sandy obliged. And now the ear spun around like a windsock. The littlest creature whirled on her hindquarters and stretched out in Sandy's direction at full gallop. Her whickering was almost lost in the wind of her own making. Now she was putting on the brakes, sliding to the fence rail, snuffling the scent to make doubly sure.

Sandy held out her hand. Twi's nose twitched, testing the salty sweat. Then she lowered her dripping head and stood stock still, clearly asking, without words, for the place behind her ear to be scratched. Suddenly she felt rambunctious and took a playful nip of Sandy's coat sleeve. Sandy's laughter cut short as quick footfalls interrupted the reunion. Kathy, all concerned, came down the steps of the house and threw her arms around Sandy. "Doctor Sandy! You're sopping wet! Come in and dry by the fire. I want you to meet my exciting guest."

"Please, Kathy, you go on in. I'll be there in a minute."

Kathy nodded in understanding and went back up the steps. Sandy reached into her pocket, took out a peppermint, and offered it to Twi, who lipped it, crunched it, savored it. Sandy started to treat the horses who had followed at a discreet distance, but Twi opened her jaws and laced back her ears. "This is *my day*," she seemed to say.

"Mine, too," Sandy replied, laughing.

At last Sandy reluctantly parted from Twi and went into the house. A fire crackling and the smell of pine smoke filled the den-size office where Kathy kept her records. An attractive stranger stood up to welcome Sandy.

"Please meet Dorita Kongot," Kathy said as she hung up Sandy's sodden jacket. "Dorita conducts a clinic for horses and trainers, and guess what? She specializes in dressage!"

Sandy liked the strength of the woman's handshake.

"Dorita was my coach," Kathy explained, "when I was a timid kid of six."

"Never timid," Dorita corrected. "I'd say quite the eager beaver! And when I heard about Twi, I gave myself a two-week leave and headed for sunny Florida." The soft patter of rain suddenly became a loud drumming. Dorita laughed. "Sunny Florida, my eye!" she said.

There were chestnuts roasting by the fire and piping hot cider, and everyone felt cozy and warm and of one mind.

Kathy kept trotting to the kitchen for more butter and passing the steaming plate of chestnuts until the atmosphere was filled with Christmas goodness.

It was Dorita with her fine understanding who reminded them of their mission. "Kathy! What Sandy wants to hear is my rating of Twi and you as a team—and Twi's Grand Prix prospects."

"Well, what are we waiting for?" Kathy rubbed her hands together. "Tell her!"

Dorita's eyes sparked to the occasion. The room went silent except for the licking of the flames. Dorita, slender as a racehorse, stood up, looking directly at Sandy. "I wish I could make you feel my deep-down satisfaction in watching Kathy and Twi working as a team."

She waited for Sandy's nod of agreement, then went on. "But for my own ego, I'm glad they both need more patient work to put them in harmony for the Grand Prix."

Sandy could feel her brows inching up in surprise. "After studying the videotape with my unprofessional eye," she said, "the action seems brilliantly harmonious . . . already close to the top."

"Oh, they are! It's that closeness I want to *seal*. When my student riders and their mounts are both in tune, there will be no need for me. That's why I'm thrilled to work on Twi's and Kathy's final polish."

Sandy caught Dorita's excitement. "Keep talking," she pleaded. "Tell me everything."

Kathy chimed in. "Dorita, tell Sandy the good stuff . . . the exciting work ahead."

Dorita nodded. "The first night here I watched the training tapes so I could zero right in on any weaknesses."

"Did you find *any*?" Sandy asked in motherly surprise.

Dorita smiled at Sandy's prejudice, while she made a point of studying Twi's encouraging award on the wall and reading aloud the golden caligraphy:

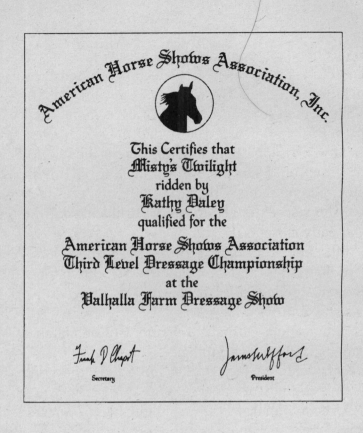

American Horse Shows Association, Inc.

This Certifies that
Misty's Twilight
ridden by
Kathy Daley
qualified for the

American Horse Shows Association
Third Level Dressage Championship
at the
Valhalla Farm Dressage Show

Frank D Chapot
Secretary

James Wofford
President

Dorita came over and put her arm around Sandy's shoulder as if she were a kid, half her age. "In dressage, we all know that the third level is an improvement over first and second levels. But we must remember that this is just a rousing beginning."

Dorita sat down in front of the fire. "What pleases me

in Twi's work is her energy, her endurance. She could go on working all day . . . if we'd let her.

"Now I'll list the things we'll be working on to put Kathy and Twi in perfect sync. First we're going to refine the basics—the walk, the collected trot, the flowing canter. Twi's canter tends to be short and bouncy, almost like an Irish jig. But we'll get to that.

"Another concern is Twi's resistance to bending left. If I knew the cause, we could work on the cure."

"I know!" Kathy exclaimed. "In her cutting career the cowboys sometimes linked her head to her tail, hoping to teach her to swerve naturally. All it did was scare her and make her resist even more."

Dorita chuckled. "Twi has such a sparkling white rump we've got to teach her to make good use of it."

"I call Twi my genius horse," Kathy said. "Although her being so wise can actually work against her trainer; she likes to outthink me. In her tempi changes, changing leads every certain number of strides, we'd be working on changes, say every four strides. Twi, on her own, might switch to three or two without any cue from me."

"She must learn to wait for your signal," Dorita agreed, "and not anticipate. That's another challenge for us to correct."

At this point the rain stopped as if a sky giant had sheared it through with a blade of sun.

"Thank you for an exhilarating session," Sandy said, "but may I come back soon to see some real action? I want to learn firsthand just how the prompting is done."

Dorita was quick to say, "Come next Saturday. We'll be taping all morning so Kathy can study the videos after I've gone home."

"I'll be here!" Sandy promised.

Chapter 20
ACTION!

A freshly raked track at sunup is almost a holy place. Hoofbeats playing soft music on wet tanbark. Barn smells—harvest hay and grains—mingling with drying compost, and over all, the pine-tree fragrance of Kritter Korner. In the ring only one splashily marked pinto pony holds center stage.

The time is mid-December. Kathy's coach, Dorita, is longeing Twi, suppling her for the work ahead. Dorita is wearing a Spanish double-pointed hat like the riders of the Lipizzaners of Vienna. Her hands on the longe line are delicately fingered, like a harpist's, ready to pluck the strings. Twi shows none of the tenseness of a beginner. Everything

is happening as it should. Dorita is asking for the basics
. . . the slow measured walk, twice around the ring; then
the trot, then the flowing canter. Just the basics. Easy as
breathing out and breathing in.

On the opposite side of the track, Sandy waves her
camera. She is ready, saving her film for Twi's performance. Kathy and Sandy are silent observers, side by
side, scarcely aware of the tourists driving through the
open gate, lining up to watch the action. The waiting is
over!

Dorita reels in the longe line. She swings gracefully
into the saddle. Effortless.

"*Now!* Sandy says to herself. "Now I shall learn the
secrets of the classical ballet—how the signals are given."

Sandy blocks out Dorita as a rider; she is like a stage
prompter in the wings. Sandy's mind is centered on
Twilight, her white spots shimmering. She is walking in
majestic dignity toward them . . . abreast of them . . . passing them, around the track once, and once again. The
pageantry flows before them, a vision of grace in action.

Then at an unseen signal, Twi's propulsion quickens.
She is up on the bit, eager, her hind legs well under her
body, her action elevated. Around the perimeter of the
track, she shows her collected walk. And then the elevated
trot. And against the unseen prompting as Twilight swings
into a canter, slow flowing at first, then faster and faster,

her tail whisking back and forth as if a turnkey is winding up a toy pony.

Sandy's camera still hangs unused over her shoulder. Her hands do not move. She is mesmerized by Twilight's elegance, the splendor of her action. But what are Dorita's secret signals? Sandy watches her knees, the calves of her legs, her hands, to catch any small movement . . . she listens to hear any clicking sound or a whispered word. She detects no prompting cues. None at all.

This was just the beginning of the miracle. Now the *passage*, a lilting trot with action so high that even while Sandy is standing motionless she has the heady sensation of scudding on a cloud. Twi is doing "the crossover," stepping diagonally forward on her tiptoes, then back again to the collected trot.

Now she is doing lead changes at the canter, changing every third stride, then every second stride, and now at every stride.

Sandy wants to catch these tempi changes. But before she can focus on Dorita's cues, the demonstration is over! Dorita slides gracefully to earth, removes her Spanish hat, and bows to the applause of the impromptu audience.

At last it is Kathy's turn. Sandy can hear Dorita's voice, full and rich, erasing any worry. Her comments are like a riding crop, full of gentle encouragement. Her directions are unique; they are not directions at all!

"Good!" Dorita stretches out the word as if it held a string of *o*'s instead of only two. "Yes! Yes! Keep sitting *in* the saddle, not on it.

"Ah, your head is up. Your heels are down.

"Go-o-od!—Your shoulders are back, your hips forward, your eyes ahead."

Dorita is running alongside now, her laughter bubbling like champagne. "Kathy, mavourneen, you are making a Lipizzaner of Twi. You are both dancing to your own music.

"You are cueing Twi like Colonel Podhajsky, the master of the Spaniche Reitschule of Vienna. You are getting her hindquarters *under* her body so she is ready to trot on air—if you ask it.

"Excellent, Kathy! Twi is obeying *your* directions, changing leads when *you ask for the change.* Tempo one! Tempo two! Tempo three . . ."

With an audible sigh, Dorita exclaims, "Yes! You and Twi are now ready to take your place in the classical world of dressage."

Kathy dismounts and bursts into laughter. She places her cheek against Twi's neck and plants a kiss on her nose. Then, with everyone turning to look in Sandy's direction, she leads Twi over to her and places a cube of sugar in Sandy's hand, giving her the honor of offering "the reward."

The excited spectators cannot bring themselves to leave. They cheer, too entranced to miss any action. Among the strangers, a red-haired tomboy and her mother hang behind.

They have a burning question.

"What," the mother asks, "is the breeding of this spunky little ballet dancer?"

Almost in concert Kathy and Sandy reply: "She's a direct descendant of Misty of Chincoteague!"

The tomboy lets out a whoop, races to the parking lot, and returns with a much-read copy of *Misty*. Carefully she flips the pages to the double spread of the ponies swimming from Assateague Island to Chincoteague. The result may have been nothing more than a coincidence, but Twi lowers her head as if to study the ponies, trying to recognize one or two old friends. Suddenly Sandy remembers to grab her camera. She focuses quickly and she snaps the scene, at the very second that the child throws her arms around Twi and tells her she is the most beautiful horse in all the world. For full seconds the child and Twi stand quietly with the book between them.

Chapter 21
HOOFPRINTS

In Twi's twelfth year, holiday time with all its family gatherings and festivities arrived with an extra flourish.

The Christmas mail brought the thrilling news that Twi would receive an All-Breeds Award from the United States Dressage Federation. As if this were not exciting enough, Sandy, Chris, and Pam all received a personal invitation. The American Horse Shows Association was inviting Twi's human family to receive a first-place trophy at the ceremony on December 27.

Sandy read the news standing up in the kitchen at the chopping block, so engrossed that she stopped nibbling the pecans she was shelling for the family's Christmas pie.

A Special Invitation for You from the . . .
American Horse Shows Association, Inc.
&
American Bankers Insurance Company

The American Horse Shows Association
and
American Bankers Insurance Company

cordially invite you to attend the

ZONE IV AWARDS BANQUET
in conjunction with the Winter Equestrian Kick-off Dance
for
Presentation of the AHSA/American Bankers Zone Horse of
the Year Awards
December 27th at seven o'clock

PALM BEACH POLO AND COUNTRY CLUB
Polo Stadium
West Palm Beach, Florida

By Reservation Only   *Please Respond*

Life certainly was sending out new challenges for Twi and for all who knew and loved her.

When Pam and Chris read the mail, Chris disappeared into the family's hardware closet, then came bounding into the kitchen with a ruler and an empty picture frame. He held the frame over the award at the point where it said:

ALL-BREEDS AWARD

presented to

MISTY'S TWILIGHT

Sponsored by the

PINTO HORSE ASSOCIATION OF AMERICA

"Wow!" Chris exulted. "The frame fits! I'll hang Twi's award in the library, right next to her picture."

"Hang it close to the oil portrait of Sunshine, her mother," Sandy added. "She'd be mighty proud of her daughter's high recognition!"

What a letdown! Sandy, Chris, and Pam never did get to the awards dinner to accept the trophy emblazoned with a gold seal and the name *Misty's Twilight.* Instead, Sandy came down with the uglies—a runny and very red nose and a scratchy throat. In a husky voice she telephoned her cancellation to the American Horse Shows Association banquet.

In her disappointment there was no hint of rejection or aloneness, no time to feel sorry for herself. Pam had flown home for the 27th of December and Chris caught a ride from The Horseman's Boys Ranch. When they saw Sandy's nose, they both cancelled their banquet reservations, too. They were so full of health and zing that the farm rang with their fun and foolishness. They put on a show of their own for Sandy. At times they were elephant and trainer; Pavarotti the elephant and Dolly Parton the trainer. Then they impersonated Mr. Rogers and Miss Piggy. Their prize performance was a rousing history of dance with Fred Astaire and Ginger Rogers. They closed with Sandy trying to carry a tune in a voice that bore no resemblance to singing!

At last the noise and hilarity leveled off with a discussion of such depth as they had not had in years.

Pam's future seemed to be laid out neatly and in order. She had graduated from broadcasting school with honors and was accepted in the fast world of movies and stage productions.

Chris still had hurdles to clear. This was no surprise to

Pam or Sandy; it was the story of his life—try this school, try that. Different schools. Different problems. But now, to everyone's joy, he had started to jump hurdles like a pro. He was working at The Boys' Ranch with outreach students. These young people were starting afresh, desperately wanting help from their peers—showing positive little beginnings and grand triumphs.

Sandy didn't know whose future thrilled her more—Pam's surefire work in the theater or Chris' understanding of the land and all of its animals. Sandy declared her pride to both. Then, to her amazement, the children turned the tables on her.

They were celebrating the last day before the new year with a late supper of waffles studded with pecans and slathered with maple syrup and blueberries. They ate in near silence.

It was Chris who broke the quiet. "Y'know, Mom, I want to talk about *you*."

Pam and Sandy exchanged surprised glances. This was a new role for Chris. His pup was nudging him, excitedly begging for the few blueberries left on his plate. Chris let him lick the plate clean, smiling at the crunching, slobbering sounds.

Neither Pam nor Sandy winced at the forbidden practice. This was a landmark moment. . . .

"I know you're a successful skin doctor," Chris began,

"but with us kids grown up, and most of the Chincoteague ponies given to young owners, what about you? Won't it be a dud just clearing up kids' faces for the rest of your life?"

"I wonder, too," Pam said. "What kind of future do you have? Of course your new flying lessons will be fun. But *where* to? And *why*?"

Sandy was taken aback at such caring. "This cold seems to make my eyes water," she said in a strangely husky voice. Then she brightened. "Actually I had planned to ask you that very question! I need your advice—not so much for myself . . ."

Chris's laughter rang out. He tapped Pam with his toe. "Remember, Pam, on the way to Chincoteague when I said to you, 'Some moms never grow up?'"

"Yeah, that was *one* time we agreed."

They all smiled knowingly. "Is it wrong not to grow up?" Sandy asked.

"No, but what about your *second* childhood?" Chris persisted.

"I'm glad you've asked, because that's the big problem, and you two have been in on it from the beginning."

Chris turned his chair around so he could lean his arms on the back of it. Pam joined the Rhodesian on the floor. Sandy fortified herself by taking some deep breaths. Then she plunged in. "It all goes back to Chincoteague."

Pam sat up. "I knew it! I knew it! It's about Misty's Twilight."

"*However* did you know?"

"Easy! When a teacher used to ask me how many children in our family, I always said three—Chris, Twi, and me. But, what about Twi?"

Sandy did not hesitate. "Twi is on the brink of greatness in her career. She may be the only pinto pony in the world to compete in classical dressage with purebred Lipizzaners and Arabians."

"Don't knock it," said Chris.

Pam turned to Sandy. "What's to worry?"

"Plenty! Is it fair to work Twi daily and strenuously, to ship her across the ocean to enter the Olympics? Are we satisfying our belief in her . . . or is it our own vanity?"

"Or what?"

"Or should she end her days being a mother, in a green pasture with thoroughbred mates and foals?"

"Why not do both?" Pam asked.

"Yeah! After collecting a bunch of gold medals, why not fly her home from the Olympics and let her be a mother? Like you! We know kids are work. But can't she handle two jobs—just like you?"

"Will you two please let me use you as sounding boards? Twilight, you see, has come to represent much more to me than gold medals and motherhood."

Chris sat up, waiting for the big question. "She's really awesome, Mom."

"Yes! And I want her to achieve all that she can. I'm proud of her, just the way I'm proud of you. But I want to go back in time for a few minutes."

Chris and Pam settled down on the floor and let their pups, Rhodi and Rags, flop down beside them.

"It has been fifteen years since the three of us went to Chincoteague, and much has changed in our world. Wild habitats, and the wild creatures they shelter, are being lost as environments change. People seem to take up more and more space, leaving less and less for creatures to exist. Isn't it important for children, the world over, to save the wilderness areas for the future of all creatures?

"Twilight has come to represent a lot more to me than a great horse with accomplishments in cutting, jumping, and dressage. She's already gone farther than any other Chincoteague pony, and I want her to go as far as she can—maybe even represent the United States as part of the Olympic team in 1996.

"However, as I think back, it is Twilight's special Chincoteague heritage—the blood of the wild ponies and the visions of wild islands with marshes, beaches, and freedom that first caught my imagination as a child and took me there with you fifteen years ago. What if all that had been destroyed—and we had never been able to share this dream?

"How wondrous life is—how precious. But it must have a chance to thrive. I would like Twilight to be a symbol for children to rally around; a symbol of what Nature has to offer us, and what we stand to lose if we aren't careful."

Pam looked thoughtful. "Y'know, Mom, maybe Chris and I didn't seem to appreciate our trip to Chincoteague, but it means a lot more to us now. We'll have kids of our own one day, and we'll want to share Assateague and other untamed places with them. We'll all have to pitch in and help!"

Thus they came back to the islands. They were no longer dots on the map, but had grown in stature because of Misty's birthright. More than ever Sandy longed to clasp both children in her arms, but she couldn't embarrass them. They were grown-up and she wasn't.

And that's the way they left it, that last day of December.

wenn horses
get ordrly
die. that
is sad but
evry but
evrybody
dies.

A Fole
is a Loy
horsia
crit her
is a Ftlly.